D1550119

THE TRUE CONFESSIONS OF A LONDON SPANK DADDY

Peter Jones

Published by Accent Press Ltd – 2008
ISBN 9781906373313

Printed and bound in the UK by
CPD Wales, Blaina

Cover Design by
Red Dot Design

AUTHOR'S NOTE

YOU PROBABLY WOULDN'T GUESS, to look at me, that I'm one of the most feared, yet sought after, men in London.

I wouldn't make any claim to being outstandingly handsome, although I am tall and dark enough. Yet beautiful women, many much younger than me, are willing and eager to give me access to their lovely bottoms. I am a Spank Daddy and my publishers have persuaded me to reveal all.

Now, before I start to recount some of my adventures for your delectation, dear reader, I think I had better set the scene a little with a few words on what people get from the spanking experience – you may be a bit mystified!

What a good spanking should achieve is a combined adrenaline/endomorphin rush, which is sometimes known as 'flying'. Flying is, I am told, better than an orgasm, but it's not easy to achieve without expertise and practice. Most women who come to me do so having tried out spanking with their husbands, finding it totally unfulfilling.

A little chemical analysis reveals what people derive from a spanking, or caning. The answer is

1

twofold – adrenaline and endomorphins. Adrenaline is, of course, a hormone created by fear and excitement, while endomorphins are a form of protein produced automatically by the body to counteract pain. The key is to build up the pain gradually, that is why school canings hurt and were never enjoyable – the pain was sudden and intense and over long before the old endomorphins got going. Endomorphins are the reason why you feel good, despite the aches and pains, after playing a sport or a trip to the gym.

The most important aspect of corporal punishment is that the spankee (the person being spanked, or caned) has to voluntarily submit, has to give up complete control, to the spanker, and have confidence and trust in him or her. The art for the (male) spanker is to take the lady exactly where she wants to go – to her limit, or even a little beyond, but not too far beyond. She doesn't want a wimp who doesn't want to hurt her because he loves her too much. (This of course is where most spouses fail.)

There is a delicate balance and one has to be able to get it right. The lady has to have confidence that you will get it right, otherwise her fear will be too strong for any enjoyment to follow. So a Spank Daddy's most important tool is his brain, he has to observe closely and know when to be more or less severe, both in word and in weight of slap, or stroke.

A most important element is that the spankee should feel that what she is getting is *proper* discipline. The limits will have been discussed in advance so that she will feel she is committed to a situation that she can't really get out of; although of course she knows she can if she really wants to.

Enough of a sense of fear has to be instilled, because that's what starts to get the adrenaline flowing, sometimes days or even weeks before the spanking takes place.

Another element in a spanking is, of course, humiliation. For a grown woman to be spanked, or caned, on her bare bottom is, by its nature, humiliating. Humiliation both increases the adrenaline flow in the spankee and helps to induce the necessary submission. A good Spank Daddy will have many subtle and not so subtle ways of making his playing partner feel humiliated before the actual spanking begins, helping the adrenaline flow and reinforcing fantasy roles.

In a nutshell: humiliation, enough fear, but not too much; enough pain, or perhaps a little more than enough, but not too much more.

Some people come to me for punishment for real-life transgressions, perhaps for cathartic release or to make a clean break from a bad habit, while others want punishment for wholly imaginary reasons, mostly linked to a fantasy. These situations often involve role-play, where a spankee who has fantasised about being caned at school might, for instance, put on her old school uniform and come to me to tell me, her headmaster, that she had been caught smoking.

People being spanked will probably, but not always, get sexually aroused. From my own experience I have to say that the spanker almost always does! Naturally a good Spank Daddy is willing to respect the wishes of a lady who does not want anything sexual to happen. Often this will be agreed in advance, although it is not unknown for a lady to change her mind about this once the session commences.

Many eminent psychologists have written volumes about the links between submission, punishment and sex, so I'm not going to go into the subject deeply here, dear reader. Suffice it to say that, if you want to improve your sex life, spanking, or being spanked, might be something worth considering!

Enough! Find a comfortable chair, loosen any tight clothing and settle down to enjoy the experiences of Peter Jones, solicitor, charmer, complete bastard and London Spank Daddy extraordinary!

TINA

NEVER DO TO OTHERS something you wouldn't have done to yourself. As a lawyer, I'm not really sure, dear reader, that I totally subscribe to this good advice when it comes to business! But, having read and digested *Screw The Roses, Bring Me The Thorns,* I realised that the world of adult erotic spanking was very different to the spanking experienced at school, so I decided that if I was serious about becoming a top Spank Daddy, I really should experience having my own backside spanked by a serious Domme.

I hoped in the process I would learn a lot about how to treat future willing spankees, from being a willing spankee myself, and, who knows? dear reader, I might enjoy it!

The idea did give me a serious thrill, especially as I knew it was likely to be seriously painful. I wanted the same sort of firm, hard caning that I had received at school, but this time I wanted to enjoy it, and also I wanted to know what a Domme would do to make it enjoyable. Interestingly, I realised that it did have to be a *she*, the thought of being caned by a man was a non-starter and still is, so for me there's clearly a sexual element. Very few heterosexual people enjoy same-sex spankings, though of course same sex-canings at school were pretty much the rule, even back then the thought of being caned by an attractive young teacher would probably have had more appeal than being caned by a gruff old man.

A little internet research was required; firstly I could well believe that most Dommes were actually rather fat and quite unattractive and those that weren't would charge a fortune – well, beyond what I was prepared to pay, anyway. Eventually the British Spanking website led me to an attractive young lady in her late twenties, who charged £50 for a no-nonsense good hiding, no sexual services whatsoever, you didn't even get to take your clothes off. Your trousers came down, your pants came down and that was that. She came heavily recommended by other guys who enjoyed a real hard-core spanking session; she hurt you and hurt you a lot. It was definitely not for the faint-hearted, but I was keen to experience the real thing and find out what made it enjoyable, what the tricks and nuances were, so I took the plunge and called her.

The first thing I learned was that the process started immediately, with the first call; 'Hello, Peter,' she said, 'my name is Tina Jennings, but you will address me as ma'am or Miss Jennings, is that clear, young man?'

I swallowed hard, this was for real, 'Yes, ma'am,' I responded, 'of course ma'am.'

'Good. Now let me explain what I do, and what I don't do, first be absolutely clear that nothing even vaguely sexual will take place, you will tell me in advance what you want and I will deliver it. I don't do safe words, there will be no going back, though I can assure you that I am very experienced and know when to stop, but you will just have to trust me on that.'

'Yes, ma'am.' I gulped again, but already I was feeling the start of an erection just from talking to the woman, she had me entranced and believing in her right from the start.

'So what did you have in mind?' she asked me. I explained that I was very scared of the thought of being caned, but that I would leave the decision as to whether I would be caned to her. In fact I would leave the whole thing to her and her judgement; I would take whatever punishment she chose to give me. Yes, dear reader, the moment I said those words I felt the same sense of fear that I had felt in my youth at school, though perhaps not as strongly, but the fear was definitely there. I also decided that I wanted her to take the decision as to when I was to be punished. We agreed that she would call me at any time of her choosing the following week and order me to go straight to her flat, near Canary Wharf. We also agreed that there would be no social chit-chat first; that I would hand her the money as a 'fine' at the start of the encounter and that she would then carry out the rest of the punishment as she saw fit.

'Next week then, young man,' she ended, knowing full well I was a good twenty years older than her. But being addressed that way didn't seem at all strange, she had me hooked.

For the next few days I thought of little else: would I be able to cope? Would it be enjoyable or would it be a painful disaster? I didn't know, and that's what I found so exciting. I lay in bed at night wondering what might or might not happen, and, in particular, when. I decided I would have to cut out drinking, as I didn't want to be punished suffering a hangover, and I would have to think about what I wore every day, in particular whether to wear Y-fronts, boxers or briefs. It was hard to decide.

On Monday morning I showered and dressed, this was the week, at any time now I could be summoned, I wasn't in control any more, she was. I was hoping it would be all over by Wednesday, but she had the option to keep me on a knife-edge until Friday night if that was what she chose. At least I couldn't imagine it would be Monday, she would be sure to keep me sweating a bit, even though I had spent the last five days sweating. Was I sane? What was the worst that could happen? I might hate it, but so what? Put it down to experience and don't do it again, but for now I knew I had to take whatever she gave me, I had no choice, I had submitted.

I had barely left the house at 8.45 when the mobile phone on the passenger seat of my car rang. Expecting a call from a client in Australia, I picked it up, but my heart missed several beats when the name Tina Jennings came up on the display. At that time of the morning perhaps she was calling to tell me something had come up and the appointment had to be postponed, or at least that's what I hoped when I answered it. 'Good morning, Miss Jennings,' was all I managed to blurt out.

'That is Peter Jones, isn't it?' I mumbled a reply. 'Please be at my apartment at 10.00 a.m. sharp, don't be early, don't be late, you know why I want to see you.'

'Yes, ma'am.'

'Then don't be late.'

'No, ma'am.' The phone clicked dead.

I felt rather shell-shocked: Monday morning and it wasn't even nine yet! The first port of call was the cash point – £50 in cash for the lady. I then drove straight to her place, arriving outside the block of flats far too early. I sat in the car for a full twenty minutes wondering why I was being quite so crazy, but I realised that actually I was excited and buzzing inside; this was quite a sexy young girl who was about to deal with me, it didn't stop me being desperate for the toilet, though, as I finally rang the bell at five to ten.

'You're early, wait.'

Five more minutes passed and I rang the bell again, this time she told me to take the lift to the fourth floor; when the lift doors opened she was standing waiting for me. Quite tall, in fact at about 5' 9" not much shorter than me, she was quite an imposing-looking girl. She was wearing a white blouse, and well-cut black trousers, every inch the serious-looking business woman. Very much the boss, she was pretty with her black hair tied back into a bunch.

She opened the door and I followed her into the entrance to the flat. 'I am going to have to teach you some manners,' she told me, 'men normally open the doors for me.'

'Yes, ma'am,' I blurted out, 'I am sorry, may I use you toilet, ma'am?'

'Certainly,' she replied, 'but be quick, knock and

come through the door at the bottom of the hall when you're ready.'

It was the kind of nervous pee that I would have experienced back in my schooldays, it took a while. Eventually I came out of the bathroom and steeled myself, very gingerly I tapped on the door, no response, a pregnant silence and I knocked again harder.

'COME IN,' came a voice from the other side. I reached for the handle and entered. It was a large lounge which contained very little furniture, though I saw with trepidation that every known instrument of punishment, straps, tawses, paddles and canes, were hanging neatly on rows of hooks on the wall. She took a cane down and showed me that it was over 4ft long, almost like a broom handle. 'This is a Singapore cane, I have only ever used it once, and fortunately for you I won't be using it this morning.'

She looked at me. 'I believe you have something for me?'

I rustled in my top pocket and took out the £50, 'Yes, ma'am, of course.' I handed her the notes.

'Face the door,' she ordered, 'put your hands on your head.' There I was, in suit and tie, 50 years old, but suddenly I was again the slightly scared schoolboy, my heart was racing but it was as much from excitement as fear, though there was definitely a mix of both.

'You are a slob, your life is a mess. Look at the state of you, you must be pretending when you go down to that gym. I'm going to punish you for that this morning and that punishment will end with 12 strokes of the cane, do you understand?' My mind raced, this was it, I had hoped she would stick with an over-the-knee spanking and a strap, but I had left the decision to her. Was I now regretting that decision? No, I thought, you're here now, no going back. And it's going to be fun isn't it? But of course, dear reader, I wasn't at all sure that it would be.

It must have been five, perhaps even ten, minutes later when she told me to take my jacket off and hang it over the back of a chair, she was seated on another chair herself.

'Undo your trousers,' she ordered. I did and they dropped to my ankles, she then tugged my boxers down and soon they were with my trousers around my ankles.

'Over my knee,' she ordered. I leant forward and laid myself across her lap, she was slim and fit with a great body, I felt a little stirring as my cock brushed against her, but it wasn't to last.

Ouch, I thought, that hurt, as her palm slapped my bottom for the first time, she means business. She continued methodically slapping each cheek in turn. Up and down for several minutes until my whole bottom must have been bright red; harder and harder the blows rained down until I was close to being unable to cope. My mind was racing again, if I couldn't deal with this, what hope did I have with what was to come? Harder and harder the slaps came down, she was a real tough cookie. I was by now emitting little squeaking noises, we had agreed no safe word, what the hell had I been thinking about? I was mad, locked in a painful situation well beyond my control, almost in tears, any more of this, I thought, and I am going to have to tell her to stop. But then she did, she stopped just before the moment where she would have pushed me over the edge. I was already beginning to appreciate her art.

'Stand against the door and put your hands flat against it,' she ordered. I had no idea what was coming next. 'Right, young man, I am going to count to ten.'

'One.' What felt like a leather paddle cracked against my buttocks, I winced audibly, the pain was intense, coming in waves with each stroke. Slowly and very deliberately she counted to ten, my buttocks were burning but this was a pleasurable burn, nothing like my first experience with the cane, though I still had that to come. I was very much aware of how much the sting lingered in the immediate aftermath of the stroke, but equally I realised how quickly it dispersed just in time for the next stroke to land. She was taking her time, that was the key, she was in total control, she had already threatened me with extra strokes for any slight act of disobedience or not carrying out her instructions to the letter.

'Turn round.' I faced her. 'Right, young man, your warm-up is over, now it's time for the serious punishment.'

Oh my God, was she serious? I had no way of knowing, she was in control.

'Get those trousers and pants out of the way.' I stumbled out of them, I was naked except for my shirt, tie, socks and shoes, I must have looked in a right state, but she was there to punish me.

She produced a tawse, which is a leather strap with a split end, around two inches wide and eighteen in length, it looked very mean indeed. 'Right, let me explain what's going to happen, I am going to give you 20 strokes with the tawse, you will count each one and thank me for it, if you forget to either count or thank me, I shall repeat the stroke, and it won't count, is that clear? When I have finished you will bend over the table and receive 12 strokes of the cane, which again you will count and thank me for, then you will be able to get dressed and go home, I will expect you back here in three months time and I will expect to see a major improvement.'

So this was it, time to see exactly what I was made of. I was by now feeling quite heady and confident that I could take it.

I leant forward against the door, resting my weight against my palms, my feet set slightly apart, aware of my balls dangling between my legs and a bit concerned she would hit them by mistake. I took a step further back so that by now I was bending more than standing. 'Let's have those feet further apart, keep going.' I shifted my feet to the point where they were a good two feet apart. I felt very exposed.

'When you are ready, Peter.' I took a sharp intake of breath, 'One, please, ma'am.' There was a loud crack of leather against flesh, arrggh, I winced, and held my breath again.

'Thank you, ma'am, two, please ma'am.' The cracking sound again, the pain erupted all over again, all I was thinking about was counting and thanking her, desperate not to make the tiniest mistake that would prolong the ordeal. I was coping with it but 20 strokes would be plenty with the cane to follow; as we got into the teens there was a definite rhythm about it that I was in control of, but it was taking a long time as I rode each stinging wave before requesting the next one.

I was feeling red raw but was quite determined to see it through. Indeed I really had to. Although there was no safe word, I knew that if I really wanted her to stop she would have to, but I didn't want her to. I wanted to see it through. 'Fourteen, ma'am.' I winced, crack! The leather struck again.

'Pardon?' she enquired. I immediately realised my mistake.

Crack. 'Fifteen, thank you, ma'am.'

'I think you will find that's still fourteen.'

'Yes, ma'am, sorry, ma'am, thank you, ma'am.' I had to get my responses right before this veered out of control; it almost had.

After twenty-two strokes of the strap I was standing again and drinking from a glass of water she had offered. Could I get through the caning without making the same mistakes? I was flying on adrenaline at this stage, and was convinced I could have taken anything at that point, Singapore cane even. But, as I learnt, that's where you get to when you're in sub-space.

'Are we going to finish this then, Jones?' My buttocks had already returned to a state of simple soreness; the waves of agony had gone, replaced only by a warm glow. But as I positioned myself across the table, hands outstretched before me, I knew I still had more to do. I couldn't see the cane but I heard her swish it a couple of times and I absolutely physically shuddered.

'We will keep it simple this time, you will count

and thank me for each stroke after I have given it, then I will decide when to give you the next one.'

Any idea I had had of being able to control things, or affect the situation, had gone: she was in total control of everything now.

There was a sharp swish and I felt the cane against my cheeks; nothing, then five seconds later it started to burn and burn some more, 'One, thank you, ma'am.' Nothing, silence.

A long pause and then, crack! It bit into my buttocks again, it was an absolutely strange sensation, deeply painful but I was flying on air and enjoying every moment as she continued to thrash me.

'Twelve, thank you, ma'am,' I cried triumphantly and it was over.

I was back in the corner desperate to rub my bottom but still following her instructions to keep my hands on my head. The pain subsided to a rosy soreness, and she told me to get dressed. I did and twenty minutes later was sitting in my car driving to the office, sore but satiated. I even decided at that point that she might have been a bit harsher, I had expected the pain to last longer. It didn't, but thankfully my bottom didn't seem to be in too bad a state.

I went straight to the toilets in the office and peeled my trousers down in front of the mirror; how wrong I was! I was black and blue and remained that way for the best part of a fortnight. It wasn't at all easy to hide it from my wife, which put me off doing it again, but it was a fabulous experience and became my template for dealing with the ladies that were to come my way in the future.

JENNY

I FIRST ENCOUNTERED JENNY Hedges in a chat-room, late one afternoon. I had been working hard all day on my own and needed a little light relief. Straight away she struck me as someone who knew exactly what she wanted, and what she didn't.

A married lady in her forties from the north of England, she was typically down-to-earth. We passed the time with the normal chit-chat and I quickly sensed that she knew a fair bit about me already. Clearly she had been talking to a friend from the chat-room with whom I had already played, and knew that I was regarded as safe and sane, always the best way to start!

She had not been into spanking for long, her husband had been spanking her for a couple of years, but she found it most unsatisfying, the old 'he loves me too much to hurt me syndrome', which is very common, and she was looking for a bigger adventure.

She had been spanked already by a few men she had met on the internet and had warmed to the experience. She had been spanked hard with a hair-brush, which she had found very challenging, though nevertheless stimulating, and she knew she enjoyed pain.

How did she enjoy the cane, I enquired, she came back that she had never experienced it. She said she was far too scared, after the hair-brush experience, but knew she 'deserved it' and would have to bring herself to face it one day. I wasn't quite sure what she meant by 'deserved it', what could a grown woman do to deserve the cane?

I gave her my phone number and asked her if she would be willing to call me to discuss her needs more fully and explain what she was talking about. Then, unexpectedly, I got the message *let me make myself a cup of tea first.*

She was gone and I thought I had blown it. I put my coat on and was ready to leave the office when the phone rang. I picked it up, expecting a business call, but instead heard a softly spoken female voice, with a Yorkshire accent. 'Is that Peter?' she asked.

'Yes, young lady,' I replied firmly.

'Oh dear,' she said, 'I can't believe I'm really doing this.'

I quickly changed the subject to put her at ease, and we must have talked for half an hour about anything and everything before the conversation returned to spanking.

'Do you cane hard?' she eventually asked, having questioned me first about my general experience.

'That's entirely up to you, young lady, I can cane you as hard or as softly as you like.' I reminded her that ultimately it was a game and she was in charge, but of course by calling her 'young lady' I was already preparing a submissive role for her – it's a good practice to establish one's authority right from the very start.

'But I don't want it to be a game,' she responded. 'I am not entirely sure if I can do this, but if I do I need you to promise me you will punish me very hard, I need to cry. I need to be brought to tears. Nothing else will do.' She went on to tell me about an incident in her life, twelve months before, when she had put her son's life at great risk, through stupidity and carelessness.

I won't go into the details, but suffice it to say that she had been a very silly girl and she was very lucky. Her husband had spanked her for it but nothing had changed, she still felt a deep sense of guilt.

From talking to some of her other spankee friends, she had decided that only a full-scale beating would provide the cathartic effect she was looking for and allow her to put the incident behind her.

Was I willing and able to provide it, if that was indeed what she wanted?

I was somewhat taken aback by the idea of a full-scale beating, but suggested to her that, within reason, I was, depending on her definition of hard punishment. If she was looking for a Singapore- or Saudi-type experience then she was crazy and I was not her man, but if she wanted an experience right up to the limit of what a genuine headmaster from the 60s would have deemed acceptable, then, yes, I felt I could deliver.

That, she told me, was exactly what she thought she was looking for, but said she still wasn't sure. She also told me that anticipation was the scariest factor for her; that I would have to get her into the mindset where it was real and not a game, and that she felt, from talking to me, and from what she had heard from others, she could trust me not to go too far.

I told her that it would inevitably leave marks that would last at least a week, or perhaps even two, which she would have to conceal from her husband, and asked her if she was comfortable about that. Yes, she was, she said quietly.

'Right then, young lady, I suggest you go away and think about this very hard. I believe you deserve something between 12 and 20 strokes of the cane, preceded by a sound hand-spanking, and you should now have no illusions about how hard it's going to be.'

'I know,' she was almost in tears on the phone, 'but I need it.'

'This is the deal, then,' I continued, 'think long and hard and then call me in my office on Tuesday morning, at 10.00 a.m. precisely, if you have decided to proceed. You will address me as *sir* and continue to do so until the punishment is complete. I will then punish you within a maximum of four weeks, and give you three or four days' notice of when the punishment will take place,' – I intended to have her like a 'cat on a hot tin roof' for the next couple of weeks – 'but please, young lady, be aware that once you have made the decision I shall carry through on what you decide, there will be no going back, do you understand?'

'Yes,' she replied, still not ready to call me sir. 'Let me think about it; it's a hunger in me.'

'Tuesday 10 a.m. then, young lady, and don't be late. The decision is yours.' And then I hung up the phone, quite convinced I had scared her to death and that would be the last I heard of it.

I was in the office for 9.30 on Tuesday, having been to the gym, and I went about my daily business refusing to get my hopes up, as I had all weekend. The clock reached 10 a.m., and nothing. Oh well. It was four minutes later that the phone rang. I recognised the number from the caller display as I picked the phone up. 'Good morning, young lady,' I ventured before she had chance to speak, 'you're late.'

'I am sorry, sir,' was the response, she had used the magic word.

'Well, Mrs Hedges,' I continued, staying in very formal mode. 'What have you decided?'

'That I do deserve to be caned, sir,' she responded, 'and I trust you to do it exactly as we discussed. Sir.'

'Congratulations, young lady,' I offered 'you won't regret it in the long term, although I can guarantee you that you will on the day.'

'When will that be, sir,' she questioned.

'When I decide, young lady, when I decide.' And I put the phone down again.

Later that afternoon, having arranged a business meeting in the north to correspond with the date I had in mind for her punishment (killing two birds with one stone!), I sent her a fairly terse email.

I was from the Crown Prosecution Service, I said and, having reviewed the files on the incident, I would be recommending prosecution and warned that she should definitely expect to serve a short prison term. However, under a new government policy being tried out, in an attempt to keep families together and the prison population down, she could instead consider the option of Corporal Punishment, twelve strokes minimum and twenty strokes maximum.

If she wished to pursue that option, I would make arrangements for our Mr Jones to visit her home one week hence at 10 00 a.m. to carry out her sentence. I made it sound like a dentist's appointment, she had said she wanted it to be real, and surely this was.

She later told me that her stomach had turned a somersault when she read it, the first of several such experiences for her over the coming week.

There was an email back the next morning, equally formal and polite, saying that she had considered the options and had decided that a visit from Mr Jones was her preferred option. Much as she feared it, she knew she was guilty and didn't want to end up in court and potentially in prison.

I emailed her back saying that she should expect a letter in the post in the next couple of days, confirming the arrangements. I then reached for my bottom drawer, inside which was a pair of proper old-fashioned school knickers I had recently purchased on ebay – just like the girls of my day were made to wear every day to school.

I popped them in a large envelope with a note:

Dear Mrs Hedges

Mr Jones will be at your home at 10.00 a.m. on Tuesday and the punishment will commence at 10.30 a.m. promptly. When you wake up you are to put on the enclosed underwear, you will also wear a skirt, with either stockings or socks, no tights.

When you get back from your school run you are to call Mr Jones on his mobile phone to confirm that your husband is at work and await his further instruction.

I hoped that the embarrassment of knowing she was wearing schoolgirl knickers at the school gate would give her a big kick. I wasn't disappointed. It did.

I sent her an email, *only six days to go, young lady, make sure you get to the post in the morning before your husband does*, I knew we were safe – he started work at 5 00 a.m.!

My excitement was building, as was hers; we had agreed not to speak again, other than by email, until the day. But I kept the emails up, and got them back, too, she had got the package and tried them on, she had also gone out and bought a cane, which her husband was due to use on her that weekend. She knew it wouldn't be great experience, but it would give her a little feel for it and, more importantly, she hoped to be able to convince her husband that he had created any marks that I had left. Devious, some women!

It got to Monday morning, *Only 24 hours to go* my email read. *I know* came the response *and I have no idea how I will get through them, I haven't slept for the last two nights and I certainly shan't tonight. This is weighing on my mind 24/7.*

I knew she was enjoying it all and that thus far I had not let her down. The sixty-four thousand dollar question was, could I get it right on the day?

I had packed my canes and strap in the car the

previous evening, I rose and showered quickly, put my suit on and was on the road heading north by 6 a.m., not forgetting to send one last email.

I am leaving home now, young lady, today's the day. Enjoy your school run, call me afterwards.

I had just left the motorway when my phone rang and I pulled over to answer it. 'Good morning, Mrs Hedges, you will be pleased to know I am making good time.'

'I'm not sure about that, sir,' she answered. I could tell, just from the tone of her voice, that she was almost quaking with fear. I prayed I wasn't overdoing it.

'Right, young lady, I shall be there in 45 minutes. I presume you are correctly dressed?'

'Yes, sir,' she mumbled.

'Then please go and place your cane on the kitchen table, once you have done that I want you to write me an essay setting out exactly what you did and why you deserve to be caned this morning. I will call you when it is time to put the kettle on.' I ended the call.

It was almost exactly 10 a.m. when I pulled up outside her door. I rang her again. 'Where are you?' she said.

'If you look out of your window,' I replied, 'you will see a red car, that's me.'

She suddenly went very quiet.

The door was opened by an extremely nervous-looking woman, 'Come in, sir, I am so glad you are here, I don't think I could have stood waiting a moment longer.'

I followed her into her kitchen. On the table was the cane with her essay beside it.

'Is that your cane, young lady? Let's see.' She passed it to me and I swished it though the air. It was very thin, very whippy, possibly hard to control.

'That should do,' I stated, 'though I may need to use my senior cane too.' She winced.

'Please, sir, no.' She knew the safe word was Peter, she only had to call me that and her whole ordeal would end instantly, but she was fully in sub mode and not taking a step back.

'Let's go through to the lounge, you can bring me a cup of tea while I read your essay.' It was still only ten past ten.

I read her essay, and proceeded to lecture her about how stupid she had been, she knew that anyway, this was the part which was very real for her. I looked her straight in the eye as I told her in no uncertain terms that she was about to receive the punishment of a lifetime and that she would certainly never be so stupid again after I had finished with her.

The clock was ticking loudly. It said a quarter past ten. 'Fifteen minutes to go until the allotted time, go and stand in the corner, face the wall with your hands on your head,' I commanded.

She complied instantly. I sat in silence, looking at her bottom in the thin floral skirt she was wearing and imagining what lay underneath. She had warned me that she was a big girl, but she wasn't really: enormous breasts yes, but a reasonably pert bottom to go with them.

This, however, was a no-sex encounter, just simple hard punishment.

I broke the silence by asking if the clock would chime at ten thirty, to signal the start of the punishment.

She turned her head to face me, 'No,' she said, 'it won't.'

I was on her in an instant, 'Did I give you permission to turn your head?'

'No, sir,' she responded.

'This will be your first, last and only warning, young lady,' I went on, 'any more disobedience from you will result in extra strokes, as we have previously agreed. You understand that, don't you?'

'Yes, sir,' she said coolly, keeping her gaze firmly on the wall in front of her.

There were five minutes to go, time to ratchet up the level of humiliation a little. I walked over without speaking and lifted her skirt, tucking the hem into the top of the knickers, which looked so magnificent on her lovely bottom.

I sat in silence again, looking at her buttocks, while she stared at the wall.

'It's almost time, young lady,' I said very softly, 'only one more minute to go now.'

It was time to start the spanking and I certainly needed to warm her up good and proper if she was to be able to take the caning I had planned for her. I sat on the sofa, 'Over my knee then, young lady,' I commanded. She turned and took up position quite quickly, skirt still tucked in her pants.

I ensured that she was in absolutely the correct position, cheeks properly presented and split, the angle so that the undersides are of the cheeks are turned upwards. Taking time to get the bottom in exactly the right place with little pushes and nudges, and positioning the knickers just so, increased her humiliation and her realisation that her bottom was now at the very centre of my attention. My left hand pressing firmly down above her waist reinforced the feeling of helplessness and submission that I wanted.

I caressed her bottom, again making sure the knickers covered as much flesh as possible, at this stage, then I slapped her quite hard, to get an instant reaction.

She winced but then settled down quickly as I rained blow after blow, reasonably gently, onto her bottom; the effect of each slap would be minimal, but cumulatively she would be slowly and surely starting to feel it.

After five minutes of this I lowered her knickers and caught sight of her quim for the first time. I had promised not to touch it, this was punishment!

I really had to get her bottom very red before she would be ready to take the cane strokes I had planned. I spanked on for what must have been ten more minutes, increasing my efforts considerably, so that my palm was getting very sore, never mind her bottom. It elicited the odd gasp, but she wasn't close to the tears she craved; this was one tough cookie.

Eventually I was satisfied and made her stand up. She was very red and had a sullen expression on her face; she knew the hard part hadn't started yet. I sent her to the other room, asked her to remove her skirt and knickers completely, and bring her husband's paddle back with her.

She returned within two minutes and handed it to me, I slapped it against my palm hard, it made me wince. And made her wince watching. I was to give her six strokes to complete the warm-up; I was about to find out how tough a cookie she really was.

'Bend over, young lady, and touch your toes,' I commanded. She couldn't quite manage it. 'I need you comfortable for this,' I stated flatly, 'just bend over and grasp the arms of the chair, but if you loosen your grip before I have finished I shall start again. I need you to keep very still, I can't safely spank a moving target.'

She was in position. I brought the paddle down on her buttocks very firmly, causing her to cry out, and I quickly followed through, whack, whack, whack, whack, whack. It was all over in seconds and she was gasping for air, her bottom quickly turning crimson, her breathing returned to normal, she was still holding the arms of the chair and not a tear in sight. They would come later, though I was going to have to work hard to extract them. A tough cookie, indeed.

Our agreement was that she was to receive 12 strokes from her nursery cane, wearing the school kickers, a proper re-creation of what would have happened at school. I would apply the strokes with near maximum force, in the event that she moved, forgot to call me sir, or forgot to count the strokes correctly, she would get an extra stroke from my senior cane, which was probably twice as thick as hers.

After a short break to allow her to compose herself, I asked if she was ready to continue. She had by now put her knickers back on and was looking at me fearfully.

'Bend over the table, young lady,' I ordered

calmly, 'place your hands in front of you, palms down on the table, with your feet about two feet apart.'

Again I spent a good three or four minutes making sure I was happy with the position, her feet ending up quite a lot further apart than I had requested, when I was satisfied I issued my instructions.

'You will remain in this exact position without moving either your hands or feet even by a fraction of an inch until we have reached six strokes, which you will be in control of by counting. When you call out the number, I will deliver the stroke, if I feel you are waiting too long between strokes I will warn you to hurry up, if you don't you will pick up an extra stroke at the end. Do you understand, young lady? Am I crystal clear?'

'Yes, sir.'

'In that case, I have to say I hope you are as scared now as your son was that morning. You certainly deserve to be.' (She later told me those words finally made her ready to burst in to tears. It was, she said, inevitable from that moment that she would.)

My final act was to pull her pants tightly up into her bum crack to expose as much flesh as I could. Her dignity was preserved but there would be little or no protection.

'When you are ready, young lady.' She got the message.

'One, sir,' she said fairly firmly, her voice very even and solid. I raised the cane and let it fly into her buttock, a perfectly aimed shot. She winced.

'Two, sir,' came within a few seconds. I raised

the cane and struck again, this time a little higher, two red weals were already forming fast. She winced again.

'Three, sir.' This time she gasped. I had caught her badly across the top of her thighs – bad practice and immensely painful.

I apologised and after a short break she announced, 'Four, sir.' I swished again but this time without the same power, it was hurting but I wasn't near to bringing her to tears. She was far too brave for that.

'Five, sir.' Swishhhhh thwackkkk came the response from the cane.

'Six, sir,' she finally gasped and the swishhh thawack came again, she had some vivid weals on her bottom and thighs now, but was still taking it well.

I needed to think.

'If you don't mind, young lady, I would like to change the plan. I cannot achieve the accuracy I need with this cane, I think I should use the senior one. In return you will get just the six more strokes with no extras, and at my pace, you won't be counting them any more.'

She spoke, 'Yes, sir, if you say so, sir, that would be a good idea.'

I left her and went to the car, the cane was wrapped in a bin bag to avoid prying neighbours' eyes. I took it in to the house and let her look at it; the length was about the same, but this one was much thicker: probably around three-eighths of an inch, possibly nearer a half, a thudder rather than a stinger.

How would she take it? Would this produce the cathartic tears she craved?

The next few minutes would tell, as she calmly resumed her position. I would strike fairly quickly this time or she wouldn't hold the position.

The first stroke made her yell, the second followed in its wake and hit the sweet spot perfectly. That must have hurt badly, but no, she was still taking it bravely.

I held back a bit with strokes three and four, knowing what was coming next, though they still made her gasp. I felt we were getting close.

I took my time with stroke five, I really had to get my aim spot-on this time, no wrapping or high or low shots. With total concentration and power I unleashed it, the swish and the crack that followed could probably have been heard in the street, the accuracy was impeccable, the effect immediate. She howled, tears coming streaming straight down her face, so I acted quickly, the final stroke was delivered within ten seconds with the same force and accuracy.

The tears became a low howl as I took her in my arms, held her tight and comforted her, telling her how brave she had been. Her red weals had turned to purple welts now, or at least the last two had.

It took, I estimate, ten or fifteen minutes for the pain level to drop below excruciating. I held her as we talked. She said that she already felt better and that the guilt had gone. We chatted for a while and then I left.

She told me later that it took her two days to be able to sit down properly and some of the marks lasted as long as a month.

Had I gone too far? No, I don't think I did, dear reader. Although she had hated the caning, she had enjoyed every moment of the build-up and everything about the release that came, once the worst of the pain subsided.

It did everything for her that she wanted it to, no pain, no gain is, I guess, the motto!

JILL

I MET JILL FOR the first time at a very smart dinner party at the Regents Park home of a barrister friend. She was an attractive-looking woman with short brown hair and glasses and a cut-glass accent. From her conversation with her neighbour at the dinner table, I gathered that she was part of the gentry, Mummy and Daddy had a big house somewhere in Norfolk at which the shooting was evidently very good.

She was wearing a fairly low cut-gown with a string of what looked to me like very expensive pearls across her generous bosom.

We had been introduced briefly before dinner but I hadn't really paid much attention to her. I noticed her glancing at me a couple of times though, and wasn't too surprised when she sought me out after we all moved away from the dinner table. My wife and her husband were helping in the kitchen when she came up to me and engaged me in some small talk. She needed to smoke and wanted to go out through the glass doors into the conservatory built on to the sitting room, which our host had told us was the permitted smoking area.

I went with her and smilingly remarked that smoking was a bad habit. Seeing her chance, I guess, she told me that she had several bad habits, in fact she used the word *naughty*! I had already guessed that she must have worked out who I was and, when she dropped the name of a friend of hers whom I had spanked a couple of months before, there was no question about it.

I looked her coolly in the eye and suggested that perhaps she needed some help with learning some discipline.

'I think you're right, Peter,' she said, or should I say *sir*?' She touched my hand lightly, her hand was cool and dry but I could feel her excitement.

'We'd better be getting back to the others,' I said, 'but here's my card, with my personal email address, get in touch if you feel I can help you.'

I didn't hear any more for a few days and it was a miserable wet January afternoon when the message from Jill dropped into my inbox. The message explained she was a sub with some experience though she hadn't played for three or four years but now she felt the need again; meeting me at the dinner party, after hearing about me from our mutual friend, had persuaded her that now might be the time. She said her married sex life was pretty non-existent – she wanted to stay with her husband but needed more. She fantasised about being used as a complete slut in every way thinkable and enjoyed a fair degree of pain.

There were just two provisos – she didn't want to be carrying marks for more than 24 hours or have penetrative sex. She'd attached her phone number, no wasting time here!

I decided the moment was there to be seized and sent her a quick text. 'Was she free to speak?' Within seconds it came back, no, but she would be when she left work at around 6.00 p.m. and I should call her then. I got back to my work, but with more than half an eye on the clock, I wanted to call her promptly when the time was right.

At precisely six o'clock I called the number, it rang a few times and then a confident voice answered.

'Good evening, Mrs King, Mr Jones here, I got your note earlier, I understand that you have been misbehaving of late and need taking in hand.' I could almost see her smiling on the other end of the phone.

'Yes, sir, you could say that.'

To which I answered, 'Well, tell me all about it.'

She clearly enjoyed the direct approach, but I quickly let it drop as we discussed everyday stuff, husbands, wives, kids, jobs, rugby. A rapport quickly developed which I think we both felt good about.

It transpired that she worked, in a very exclusive estate agency, no more than three stops away on the underground from me. She had a very busy life, often worked long hours, and was looking for a guy to escape to, perhaps once a month, to be used, abused and spanked. She really didn't want much contact at all between sessions, she didn't want it impinging on her upper-class lifestyle.

It was quickly agreed that we should meet again. She understandably didn't want to play on first meeting, but she wanted a binding commitment from both of us that, if things went well, we would play very quickly. We agreed to meet at my local pub, near the office, on the following Wednesday, with the understanding that she would be spanked on the Friday evening if all went well. The spanking would take place at my office after the cleaners had done their rounds.

She explained that she needed to be put in the mindset where this was not a game and very much for real, though of course we would have our safe word.

On Wednesday morning she called me, saying it looked like she could get off work early and suggested we bring the pub meeting forwards to four o'clock. I agreed. I was, I hoped, looking my best, suited and booted, collar and tie, ready to go – the perfect Headmaster figure.

She was looking even more attractive than I remembered her from the dinner party, and was extremely smartly dressed. I have no objection to posh girls, within reason, and she was well within the realms of reason. Conversation quickly turned to what turned her on, she enjoyed being spanked and was happy to take the cane too, if I was careful not to mark her. Sexually, I could do anything bar penetration. I was free to play with her, no holes barred, and she was more than happy to give me a blow job, if that was what I wanted.

'Right then, young lady,' I said, taking the reins again. 'Friday night it is at 7.30 p.m. sharp. You've been a filthy slut and you will pay the price. Do you have a problem with that?'

'No, sir,' she whispered back.

'Right,' I said, 'let's go. Before you head for home I want to quickly show you my office, so that you know where to come, you don't get lost and you're comfortable with the surroundings.'

We walked fairly slowly back to my office, which was less than a hundred yards away. Reception was shut so we walked up the stairs to my office on the fourth floor. She followed three or four steps behind without speaking. It was already early evening.

I unlocked the door and she followed me in. I gestured her to sit down and sat down myself behind my desk. I was fully switched to Dom mode now.

'Right, young lady, this is the office, this is the desk you will be bending over on Friday evening, and it will hurt, are you ready for that?'

'Yes, sir,' she said quietly.

'Do you have any questions?' I asked.

'Yes, sir,' again she spoke quietly, 'where do you keep your cane?'

'Behind the filing cabinet over there,' I explained, pointing. 'Away from the prying eyes of cleaners, visitors and my PA.'

'Can I see it?'

'Certainly, young lady.' I had to get down on my hands and knees but eventually fished it out, slightly taken by surprise at the turn of events.

I stood up and flexed it in my hand, it was a genuine school-issue rattan cane dating from the 60s that had no doubt seen active service in some school somewhere, crook-handled, around 30 inches in length and a quarter of an inch thick.

'See,' I said, 'not too scary, is it?' She was silent. I looked her in the eye and cracked it quite hard against the back of my leg. I almost winced.

'You see,' I said, 'it doesn't hurt that much, and

barely leaves a mark.' I lifted my trouser leg and showed her a red mark that was already fading; I knew I had her confidence now.

She spoke again, with a smile on her face, 'Would you like to use it on me, sir?' 'Now? Are you absolutely certain?' I asked.

'Yes.'

'Don't forget,' I said, 'all you have to do is call me Peter and I will stop immediately, but for as long as you are calling me Sir, or Mr Jones, I shall treat that as your continued consent – even if you are begging for mercy.'

She smiled at me again. 'Yes, sir, I know that.'

'Well in that case, young lady, you need to wipe that smile off your face, go and stand facing that door, you should lock it first, and then place your hands on your head until I am ready for you.'

She did as instructed, I sat quietly at my desk for a couple of minutes and watched her. We were in play...

The silence was complete, as it should be at these times of reflection for a naughty girl awaiting her punishment. Eventually I stood up and cleared the surface of my desk, placing a cushion on it, and a chair for her to kneel on. I then placed both the tawse and the cane at the end of the desk.

She turned to look, to see what I was doing. I spoke very firmly, 'Did I tell you to move?'

'No, sir,' she whispered.

'Then I suggest you learn to follow my instructions, or you will find this experience considerably more painful than you had imagined.'

She was wearing a white blouse and black culottes. After about ten minutes of silence I was ready.

'Could you take your blouse off please, young lady, hang it on the chair, and then return to position.'

She did. Her breasts were magnificent. I was starting to enjoy this.

With her hands still on her head, I moved over and undid the clasp of her bra, she didn't move. I then took it off completely, instructing her to remain where she was. I took my leather cuffs and attached one to each wrist in turn. She didn't flinch. Then I attached the two cuffs together with a clip.

'Right, you slut, turn round,' I said firmly, 'let's see those breasts of yours.'

She turned with her hands secured behind her. I was surprised to note that her splendid breasts were pierced and had what looked like a small metal bone passing though the nipples. I couldn't resist the temptation to take one in each hand and play with them; until the nipples were rock-hard and the size of cherries.

'I suggest, if you're going to be a slut,' I told her, 'you be my slut, and no one else's.'

I picked up the tawse and tapped it against my palm.

'Right, young lady, let's get started.'

I undid the button on her culottes and let them fall to the ground, exposing lacy black French knickers.

I quickly undid the cuffs so that she could put her hands in front of her and then recuffed her.

'Kneel on the chair and then bend forward over the desk, until your nose touches it,' I ordered. 'That is your position and you will keep it. If you don't the consequences will be very painful. Do you understand?'

Having felt the curve of her bottom, I hitched the knickers up as far as I could to expose as much bare flesh as possible. I started with twenty little flicks with the strap in rapid succession. None would have hurt and it was all over in about thirty seconds. I heard a definite 'Ooh' at the end and knew she had enjoyed it because I could see her panties moisten.

'Let's have these down, then,' I said, pulling her panties down to her knees. 'This time it's going to hurt, I want you to count to twelve for me.'

Taking careful aim, I wrapped the tawse across her buttocks carefully avoiding her hips. My stroke was perfect. She winced slightly as a bright red mark quickly appeared in the shape of the tawse, two-tailed with each tail tapering to a point.

'One.'

I laid the tawse on again, directly above the first stripe.

'One what, young lady?'

She said nothing, I laid on a third stroke.

'You need to learn some respect, young lady. One what?' The penny dropped.

'One, sir,' she said, 'sorry, sir.'

'This could be a very long afternoon if you are not careful,' I chided her.

'Yes, sir.'

I slapped the tawse against her reddening buttocks again.

'Two, sir,' she said quietly.

I continued this for several minutes, leaving about

sixty seconds between strokes, just time for the pain to build and subside before the next one. With each stroke her gasp became a little stronger. It was certainly a gasp of pleasure though, not of pain.

We got to ten, and I announced that she didn't need to count the last two strokes, they would be given in quick succession, and be far harder than the strokes to date. I aimed carefully and struck hard, two strokes seconds apart. She winced and groaned very audibly, gasping as the pain of the strokes soared to a peak as it does about thirty seconds after the stroke is given. I suspected the gasp was an orgasm so reached my hand between her legs and inserted two fingers into her dripping pussy.

'You enjoyed that,' I said, 'didn't you? Let's see what you make of the cane now, but first, get back to the corner. Now.' She retreated to the corner and I sat back watching her redden. It looked fine. No sign of any bruising, just very red, very sore but it would be gone by the morning.

I flexed the cane in my hands again, the time had come, I left her for about ten minutes more to stew in her own juice, then asked her to turn and face me. She wanted to be told off now; she was going to get it.

'Right, Mrs King,' I said fixing her with my eye. 'You know why you are here. Girls who mess around can expect serious consequences when they are found out. You're lucky that I am not going to tell your husband but I am going to make sure you can't sit down for the next couple of days. Is that understood? You can stop me at any time that you feel you can't go through with it, but you're a naughty, filthy slut and you know you deserve this.'

She eyed me back, genuinely nervous now, not knowing how hard I was going to cane her, but knowing that I was very serious and that this was the point of no return.

'I understand, sir, I will take the cane, sir,' Her voice was trembling, only slightly, but very definitely trembling.

'Bend over then, young lady, and touch your toes,' I almost barked this time. She struggled to touch them.

'Not very fit are we, young lady? You'd better grasp your ankles instead.'

This she managed and I was treated to the most glorious view of her quim, lips glistening, moist and inviting. It was made for a cock to be thrust inside but I had made a promise, so as I focused on the matter in hand, my erection subsided slightly.

The first stroke produced an audible wince, and once again I waited for the pain to peak and pass before delivering the second stroke. And the third and the fourth. By now she was gasping again, and rocking back and forwards, I didn't want her to fall so made her bend over the desk. This time there was no chair and I positioned her feet a good two feet apart.

'Keep very still or you will get extra strokes,' I barked. By this time I was worried about potential marking so I made sure I didn't up the tempo any more. I'm sure she would have enjoyed it, but I had made a promise. As I continued, her gasps were replaced by involuntary cries of 'Ouch' as she desperately fought to remain composed and not move. As the heat of the final stroke subsided, I acknowledged she had been a brave girl while inwardly reflecting that she wouldn't want to sit down on the tube home to South Kensington.

I had however one last move to surprise her with before our play session was complete.

'Do you want to be my slut, then?' I enquired.

'Yes please, sir,' she almost purred.

I cuffed her again this time with her hands behind her back. She was completely naked. I asked her to kneel in front of me and she obliged, I hadn't told her about the leather blindfold I had in my drawer but I quickly produced it and, without a word, covered her eyes. I stood up and removed my shoes, trousers and pants. Seating myself in the chair I grabbed her very firmly by the hair, not enough to hurt, but enough to hurt if she resisted.

I was in control. I guided her head over my cock and thrust deeply, this wasn't a blow job, I was fucking her mouth. She turned out to be an expert, taking me deep inside and licking the tip of my circumcised cock in turn. It was wonderful.

I was deciding what she did, and when, so when I was ready to explode I simply took it out and made her lick my balls instead. I watched my desk clock, determined to make it last as long as possible. She was in darkness, lost in sub space, happy to grant me my every pleasure. I entered her mouth again and eventually it all got too much. I came and as I withdrew my seed shot all over her face and dripped from her chin.

I released her and hugged her and then we both dressed quietly. She was smiling.

'I really enjoyed that,' she purred, 'especially the

blindfold, I never expected that.'

'So did I,' I said truthfully, 'can I buy you another drink?'

ANDREA AND SIMONE

I HAD BEEN LOGGING onto the website Facebook for a while, not as myself, you understand, but under a pseudonym, and had got engaged in all kinds of email chat and banter, with a wide variety of girls from across the globe. But, by and large, none of them seemed particularly serious. I had met and spanked one lady, but she was someone I already knew from another site, so I am not sure that counts as a Facebook spanking. In general the girls were young, far too young for me; I had set myself a lower limit of 30, well perhaps 28, below which it simply didn't feel right. There are plenty of thirty-something fish in the sea to keep me happy, dear reader, and I was equally content playing with ladies in their 50s. It gave me a wide and varied choice of partner, and left me feeling sorry for those older ladies who felt uncomfortable playing with younger men; or were unable to find one if they wanted to. It's so much easier being a middle-aged man than a middle-aged woman, I am sure.

None of this prevented me from getting contacts and requests to become friends from all manner of young ladies, none of whom I would have felt really comfortable playing with. I am sure most were simply teasing me anyway, but one Facebook group for Girls Who Enjoy Being Spanked did turn up all sorts of wannabes, most of whom had no clear idea of what they wanted, or what to really expect if they found it.

One or two, though, became quite persistent, not understanding why at 21, 23 or 25 no one older would take them seriously. Their boyfriends had probably spanked them, but they had found that unfulfilling and were really intrigued by the idea of being spanked, caned even, by a chap old enough to be their real-life father or headmaster.

One girl who was particularly persistent was an attractive young thing of 23, clearly very well educated, with a first-class degree in History from one of the better universities.

Who was I to tell her that she wasn't mature enough to make her own decisions about what she wanted to experience, she demanded in one of her emails, her arguments became quite persuasive and eventually, in a moment of madness, I succumbed and gave her my phone number. Maybe that would be the last I would hear of her, I thought; picking the phone up is always the hardest part. It was a Wednesday, and by Friday I had heard nothing, another trail gone dead, probably for the best this time! It was early afternoon on the following Monday when the mobile phone I kept strictly for contacting the spanking world rang. I wasn't particularly expecting a call – who could it be, I wondered.

'Hi!' The voice sounded chirpy, 'Is that Peter?'

'Yes,' I replied, 'it most certainly is, whom am I

speaking to?'

'It's Simone,' came the response, which really had me racking my brains, I didn't know any Simone. After a pause she explained, 'You don't know me, I'm Andrea's partner.'

'Andrea's partner?'

'Yes,' she replied, 'did she not tell you she was bi-sexual?' No, she hadn't and I was taken slightly aback. 'We've been talking over the weekend. Andrea is very keen to meet you, and in honesty I am too, and someone needs to hold her hand and make sure she is safe.'

At this stage I think I was more worried about these girls than they were about me, this was too much like every man's fantasy; what kind of a trap was it? Should I take it at face value, or run? I asked her how old she was. 'Oh, 26,' she breezed, 'if you're asking, and, before you ask, I am submissive as well. We rather like the idea of being spanked together by an older guy who is of no sexual interest, and we think you fit the bill.'

I was unsure as to what kind of back-handed compliment that was, but equally at least I understood her, or their, motives very clearly, and the idea was starting to have its appeal. I could hardly be accused of molesting girls who were self-confessed Lesbians, this would be a new experience – probably not one to be repeated. I was still very wary, though, and wasn't going to rush in as I might have done with older girls. 'Why don't I buy you girls a drink?' I suggested and we agreed to meet on the Thursday evening in El Vino's by Blackfriars Bridge, a perfect place for a mature gentleman to lead two young fillies astray.

*　　*　　*

I arrived a few minutes late, the underground playing up as usual, and I spotted them straight away, sharing a bottle of white wine. I introduced myself, we kissed on the cheek, and I headed for the bar to treat us to a second bottle, returning to them through the throng some five minutes later. They were both very different: Simone was tall and auburn-haired, slim and very classily dressed, almost a throw-back from the twenties or thirties in her tight black skirt, you could see she had made an effort. Andrea, the younger girl, by contrast, had clearly rushed there straight from work, from somewhere pretty laid back. She was short, no more than 5' 2", with shoulder-length blonde hair, and was very simply dressed in jeans and a white T-shirt, she was bra-less – I could just make out the nipples on her tiny breasts – she was quite gorgeous.

'Well, young ladies, you are clearly more serious than I thought, do you really want to be spanked by a chap like me?' I smiled at them, 'Now you have met me in the flesh?'

'We certainly want to know more about you, now we know you're so good-looking!' replied the older girl. Flattery has never offended me so we proceeded to spend the next couple of hours chatting, me telling them stories of my youth and what it really was like growing up, when corporal punishment wasn't an optional extra, but was something that you had to behave seriously well to avoid. Simone told me some stories that her mother had related about life in her public school back in the late 60s and Andrea told me how her father had often threatened to spank her, but Mum had always stepped in and grounded her instead,

48

leaving her wondering exactly what it would have been like if Daddy had kept to his word. Surely, she mused, being spanked was preferable to being grounded for a couple of weeks, surely it couldn't hurt that much. I assured her that sometimes it could, especially if the cane was brought into play. I warned them both that they were playing with fire, if they wanted to experience what Simone's mother had experienced at school.

'If that's what you want girls, then I can oblige you, but, as they say, be careful what you wish for!'

We also got into a discussion about the *when* and the *why*: the *why* was simple, they shared a flat that they both knew was normally a filthy hovel, with days of washing up stacked in the sink, and clothes everywhere. They had forgotten what the hoover was!

The *when* they would leave to me, it would they both thought be so much more interesting if they didn't know quite what to expect or when. As we parted into the night, them heading for Whitechapel, and me back to North London, Simone handed me a slip of paper with their address on, 'When you're ready, sir,' she murmured and off they went, leaving me wondering what I had let myself in for and how I should play it. I certainly had to manage this one carefully, no plunging in but taking it in stages.

But the best-laid plans …

The weekend passed and I formulated my plan. At four o'clock on Monday afternoon I phoned each girl in turn, 'I hope you have cleared the flat up over the weekend as I asked', I announced, 'I shall be with you at 7.00 p.m. for my inspection and you're for the high jump if you disobeyed me!'

Simone took it in her stride but Andrea sounded a little distressed, 'I'm meeting a friend after work,' she explained, 'can't we make it eight? I still have some tidying to do.'

I was unimpressed, 'Seven o'clock, young lady, seven o'clock, you have had more than enough time.'

I arrived at their flat and knocked on the door at around seven-thirty, deliberately late. That night both girls were in jeans and T-shirts, looking as if they had been working hard. Andrea answered the door, looking as gorgeous as ever, but immediately I felt a little twinge of guilt; she was a couple of years younger than my eldest son, and only slightly older than my daughter.

I had a cane secreted in my overcoat, hidden from prying neighbours. As we went into the lounge, which was by now immaculate, I took it out, 'I have a present for you, girls, you haven't seen one of these before, have you?' I swished it through the air, causing Simone to take a step back with a start.

'Peter, I didn't think you were going to cane us tonight!' She had safe-worded me immediately, and the truth was I had no intention of caning them anyway, that might come later.

'Don't worry, ladies,' I replied, 'I know you won't have let me down tonight, but just to make sure that you are in no doubt as to the fate of disobedient young ladies, I intend to leave this here. I suggest we hang it in the wardrobe, as a reminder of what will happen if you fall back into your slovenly ways.'

'The lounge looks immaculate, by the way. I am

impressed. Are you going to show me round?' The small kitchen, on the face of it, was equally impressive, though Simone winced slightly when I opened the cupboard door and spotted a thick layer of spilled sugar on the middle shelf.

'I didn't quite have time, sir,' Andrea said quickly, 'we'll have it finished soon.'

'Soon!' I glared at her, 'Don't you mean soon sir?'

'Yes, sir, I guess I do,' she answered, and shot back into the lounge and sat down.

I followed her and sat down, Simone followed me in with a tray of coffee, and we chatted some more. 'If this place was as bad as you said it was, I'm impressed. I can't see any reason even to spank you tonight, you must admit, though, that I am a good motivator. Would you have done this had it not been for our chat on Thursday evening? I very much doubt it.'

It was a one-bedroom flat, all on one floor, with the bedroom door leading off from the lounge. It suddenly struck me, as I was thinking of leaving, that I hadn't checked it out. The cane was lying on the coffee table; I turned to the older girl, 'Pick the cane up Simone, let's go and find a home for it.' She picked it up and held it, flexing it gently in her hands. She had confessed to having a slight Domme tendency on the Thursday, I knew she had spanked Andrea herself but never very hard, only as part of their love-making.

'Come on, the pair of you, I need to get moving.' Andrea had a distinctly worried look on her face as she opened the door and as I stepped into the room I understood why. 'What on earth is this? What's been going on here?'

It looked as if a bomb had struck, the large double bed was made, perfectly, and to the right-hand side of the room, it was fairly tidy, I say fairly tidy, but only in relation to the other half of the room that had clothes and make-up strewn everywhere, there was even an empty vodka bottle on the floor.

'Looks like someone still has work to do. Who is responsible for this?'

Andrea actually raised her left hand, 'Me, sir, I guess.'

'And why,' I turned to Simone, 'didn't you help her? I told you I was holding the two of you jointly responsible for the flat, and didn't want one person blaming the other.'

They looked at each other, not sure what to say next, I looked at Andrea, 'Young lady, this will be the last time this happens, if I ever come to this house again and find it in such a state, you will be feeling the cane and it wont be open to discussion. Is that understood?'

'Clearly, sir,' replied Andrea. I looked Simone in the eye, 'Yes, sir,' she replied, 'we both understand.'

'I am going to deal with you tonight,' I said, 'but let's do something with this cane first. I presume no one but you two comes in here?' I asked.

'No, sir, very rarely, why do you ask?'

'Pass me the cane,' I ordered. Simone put it in my hand, I walked over and shut the bedroom door. As I expected there were clothes hooks on it. I hung the cane on the middle hook, 'That, ladies, stays there – a constant reminder of who I am and what I mean to you.'

I sat on the edge of the bed and looked at them; both staring at me. 'Right, ladies, before you decide I am completely soft, which of you two is going over my knee first?' I reached inside my suit jacket pocket and pulled out my tawse, which was over twelve inches long and two-tailed: each tail was three-quarters of an inch wide. 'This will serve our purpose tonight.'

'Simone, come here, Andrea, face the door hands on head; you are the more culpable, so I will put Simone out of her misery first.'

With Simone standing in front of me, I unbuttoned and unzipped her jeans; as I pulled them down to her knees her pink cotton panties came down with them. I took her left hand and gently pushed it up her back, forcing her into the bending position as I did so. She went over my knee without a struggle and it struck me immediately that, although I found the sight attractive, she would be reacting in much the same way to me as I would to being spanked by a man. I set about my business with considerable gusto, spanking each cheek hard in turn, two minutes and perhaps eighty or a hundred spanks later, my hand was sore and her cheeks were bright red. I made her lie face down on the bed, and then called Andrea over. She was close to tears, and shaking, 'Now come on, Andrea,' I chided, 'you're responsible for getting the pair of you in this mess, I hope you are not going to balk at your punishment?'

Her jeans weren't quite as tight as Simone's so, when I hauled them down to her knees, her knickers remained in place. A deft flick of her arm up behind her back and she also was quickly in position. I pulled the knickers up tightly into her crotch and set about the spanking with equal gusto, within a minute she was sobbing, by the time I had finished she was bawling her eyes out.

'Not quite as brave as your friend here, are we?' I commented as I made her lie down next to Simone, face down, bottom up, in the space I had just vacated. I tugged at Simone's jeans until they were off completely, folded them neatly and laid them on a chair by the side of the bed. 'That, young lady, is how you treat clothes and unless you want to feel my cane you will remember it.' Within a minute Andrea's jeans were off and folded too. As they lay on the bed, neither wearing more than a T-shirt, reddened bottoms in the air, I noticed that they had joined hands and were squeezing each other tight for comfort; I let them get on with it. But not for long.

'Let's have you both up on your hands and knees,' I suggested quietly and firmly, 'and then we can get this done with.' Both had firm buttocks and thighs and a softness of skin that I had not experienced for a good few years. I didn't want to put these girls off. I took the tawse in hand and walked to the side of the bed, I gave Simone two swift strokes, enough to sting but not enough to bruise, and then slowly and deliberately walked around to the other side of the bed, where I did the same to Andrea, but perhaps a little more softly this time. I could see she was a delicate petal who needed to be trained gently.

'I will be back one day next week to check you out again, I hope you've learned your lesson!' And with that I turned to go.

'Just a moment, sir,' Andrea said.

'Yes, young lady?' She had a quick whispered conversation with Simone, who nodded back at her.

'Well, sir, we realise that this hasn't been a very pleasant experience for you, and we're very grateful. We were wondering if … if we could do anything for you?'

'Yes, sir,' Simone chipped in, 'and, looking at the bulge in your trousers, perhaps there is something we could do!'

As you can well imagine, dear reader, knowing me as you now do, she was correct about my trousers. I was rather startled as I genuinely had had no expectation of any sexual action with these girls. I remembered that Simone had told me that I wasn't of any sexual interest, but then of course they hadn't met me at that stage and been captivated by my charm! I'd been thinking of them as Lesbians but, I remembered, Simone had said that Andrea was bisexual.

I had to think quickly, I was certainly aroused by the thought of having sex with two women together, but I knew that I risked getting into a situation I wouldn't be able to control. Simone might get jealous, might go to my wife … thoughts raced through my mind.

However, the one thing I couldn't afford to do was to lose my authority by dithering and appearing weak and indecisive. What the hell, I decided!

'Possibly there is, young lady, but I'm not at all sure you deserve any pleasure. In any case, I don't have any condoms.'

Andrea giggled, opened a drawer on the bedside table and fished out a packet of three.

The minxes had planned this all along! It

reassured me that, if they had planned in advance to have sex with me, Simone must have been OK with it.

They were both still lying face down on the bed, looking at me over their shoulders.

'Simone,' I said, 'you may get up from the bed. Come here. You, young lady, remain in position.'

She got up, naked from the waist down and walked over to me. I quickly kicked off my shoes and removed my socks. 'You can undo my belt.'

She unbuckled the belt and my trousers slid down, I stepped out of them and my cock tented out the front of my Y-fronts. 'You may now remove my underpants.' I wanted to see if she showed any interest in touching my cock. If she did then I planned to involve her in a threesome; if she didn't then I would just make her watch while I screwed Andrea.

I needn't have worried, as she drew the pants down below my thoroughly rampant member she moved her head forward and gave it a kiss, right on the tip, licking off a spot of pre-come which had formed. Andrea gave a little gasp.

'You may put a condom on it.' She did this by forming her mouth into a small 'O' putting the condom in it and using her lips to unroll it down the length of my cock – a trick I hadn't come across before.

I removed my shirt. 'OK, young lady,' I said to Andrea, 'you may move down the bed towards me a little, but maintain your position. If you wish you may remove your T-shirt.' She did, and Simone followed suit, I was naked in a room with two beautiful naked young girls. Remember this, Peter, I said to myself!

I instructed Simone to get on the bed underneath

Andrea in the soixante-neuf position, she did and they both looked at me.

'Ladies, you may now do what comes naturally!' I had had enough of issuing instructions and decided to let things develop as they may.

Andrea now had her face buried in Simone's crotch. I knelt behind her, lifted up her poor red and sore bottom and impaled her dripping cunt with my cock. Simone licked and sucked my balls every time my stroke brought them in range of her mouth.

I won't weary you with all the details of what we got up to, dear reader, suffice it to say that Simone turned out to be bisexual too!

After we had finished and got cleaned up, the girls went and made me a cup of coffee.

When they came back, Simone had clearly been elected spokeswoman. 'We hope you don't mind, sir,' she said, 'but we want to look upon tonight as a one-off. It was great but we really are happy just with each other. We would still like you to help us with discipline, but nothing more.' They looked at me, perhaps expecting me to be angry, but of course I couldn't have been better pleased. I wouldn't have to get involved more deeply than I wanted to and I could still look forward to spanking their pretty bottoms.

'Very well, young ladies,' I said. 'You can rely on me.' I paused. 'In fact you can rely on me to make the punishment you received tonight look like a vicarage tea-party unless this place is cleaned up before my next inspection!'

I dressed and left them and went home. I had to remind myself when I got home not to keep grinning like the cat that had got the cream, I didn't want my wife to guess what I had been up to!

ANGELA

I HAD BEEN EXCHANGING emails with Angela for the best part of eighteen months with absolutely no sign that she was ever going to be more than an entertaining tease. She appeared to live somewhere in rural Suffolk, though it might have been Essex she didn't really say. She was stunningly good-looking, if one believed the photo was really her, she had a tall dark wealthy husband and three gorgeous young kids, and an idyllic lifestyle in what I imagined to be a country manor. But, then again, one wasn't really to know whether it was true or not; she seemed to spend an awful lot of time almost every other weekend gallivanting into town to attend all-night fetish clubs, or so she would have had me believe. All in all, one hell of a lifestyle for a late thirty-something, so I mostly took it with a pinch of salt.

She was, however, a wonderful internet flirt, and she would often email me telling me how naughty she had been. I, in turn, would from time to time suggest we had lunch together and a spot of spanking, but at the eleventh hour it never came to anything. She couldn't risk marks, her husband would dump her instantly if he ever got wind of what she was up to, so everything between this lady and myself seemed destined to remain in fantasy land; but it was a fun fantasy and we kept it up.

I did get a message from her briefly to say that she was in terrible trouble with her husband; they were trying to patch it up, and she was disappearing off-line for a while if not for ever. This was quite normal, people disappear all the time then reappear with a new persona, that's the internet, rather like the dodgy company directors I come across at work so often, dear reader!

I thought no more about it until when, a couple of weeks later, I got into my office one morning and found a note in my inbox. As soon as I saw the name I realised that it was the husband – my God, I thought, what am I going to be accused of now – I hope he doesn't think I am a real part of her fantasy world. It could be like being at school, getting caned for something you hadn't done, on very circumstantial evidence.

I opened the email and read it.

Dear Peter,

Forgive me for writing, but I am aware that you have been in touch with my wife for some considerable time, I am less than happy about that but I know you have never met and she has done far worse things than chat to you, I am contacting you because, having scoured her inbox, I have finally concluded that she is genuinely more scared of you than anyone else, I have spoken to her about this and she said that it was all a game, and you were certainly not a game she would want to play in real life. Unfortunately the games I have found out she does like to play include cavorting in clubs till all hours of the morning in varying states of undress while I am away on business and she has my mother at home looking after the children. I know she has also been involved in affairs with four or five guys almost simultaneously over the last three years, and those are only the ones I know about. I pretty much decided to leave her, but after three weeks of interminable rows she has convinced me that I should find another way to punish her, and that she won't venture out of my sight again. I am inclined to believe that she is generally remorseful and I do have the children to consider, but I don't feel I can let her get away with it, so it struck me over the weekend that you could be my solution. I haven't discussed this with her and I don't intend to. I simply want you to turn up at our house and thrash her in my presence, none of this safe word stuff, which I understand is normal, you will thrash her until I and I only decide that she has had enough. I am sure that you will enjoy every moment and she won't, neither will I, particularly, but at least justice will have been done and I hope the air will be cleared.

Please give me a call on this number to discuss further.

Regards

Roger Pendleton.

I was, I think if you will excuse the vulgar expression,

gobsmacked, but immediately realised that, as attractive as the proposition was on paper, I could have no part of it. What was this chap doing going through her inbox in the first place? He was clearly no angel, and what he was suggesting was without doubt non-consensual and bordering on assault. I wasn't planning to spend six months in a prison cell for this man, no matter how attractive his wife was. I quickly emailed him back and told him so; assaulting people against their will was not something I was into. If we were to make any progress he had to first tell Angela of his plans, and she had to agree. Secondly, only I would decide how hard to punish her, only I would decide when she had had enough.

I needed to know she was consenting, even if there was an element of coercion involved, I appreciated the fact that she had been a very silly girl. I also blind copied her in on the reply and his initial mail, so that she would know what the score was, I imagined she wasn't going to be pleased.

It was several hours before I got her response, she simply asked for my phone number again. I emailed it back to her and a few moments later my phone rang, a softly spoken girl with the slightest hint of a French accent was on the other end of the line.

'Hi, Peter, we meet at last, this is Angela, I never imagined we would ever get to speak.'

'Neither did I, young lady,' I responded, trying to start off on just the right note. 'You have got yourself into a mess here, haven't you? I am guessing a lot of what he's saying is true. I was always fairly sure you were making it up, was I wrong?'

'Unfortunately for me, yes, and unfortunately for me a female friend of his spotted me at Torture Garden three weeks ago and spilled the beans. I am not convinced he's not having an affair with her too, the spiteful cow, but for now it's me who's in trouble, and you are going to have to help me. I am going to have to go through with this – hell, it's something I have always fantasised about, without ever dreaming I would actually do it, now I don't have a choice. Please, Peter, do as he asks. I want to go through with this, well, I don't, but I have to, but please don't tell him we have spoken, just let him keep the belief that it's all his idea and all a big surprise.'

'Whooooaa, Angela, this is all a bit over the top for me, I am not going to thrash you at another man's behest. I will give you a good old-fashioned school caning if you want and send you home in tears, but I am not drawing blood or leaving you scarred for life. I have to be the one in control, not him, for the safety of both of us.'

She agreed with me and when she asked how we could do it, it almost sounded as if she was going to burst into tears. 'I don't know,' I responded, 'give me an hour and I'll call you back.'

We rapidly hatched a plan, he would be kept in the dark that it wouldn't come as a surprise to her, as long as he agreed that I was in control.

I emailed him back and blind copied her again.

Dear Roger,

On reflection, I can understand what you are trying to

do and I can see it's no less than she deserves. I am quite happy for you to keep the element of surprise if you are prepared to give me control, my being in total control is my only pre-requisite. If you tell me when and where I am happy to turn up and surprise her. I will tell her why I am there and what I am going to do, if she chooses to send me away, I shall leave, and you will have to deal with in your own way. I am not going to punish her against her will, if, however, she agrees, as I sense she will, then I will spank her first and then give her twenty-four strokes of the cane, hard enough to bruise but not hard enough to cut or scar. I normally cane on the bare, so that I can see what I am doing. Once I have finished I will leave, however you have to promise me that you will forgive her and not hold her recent misdemeanours against her.

If you are happy with my proposal then you only need to provide me with an address and time. Lunch time or early afternoon on Saturday or Sunday would be ideal for me.

Regards

Peter

The response came quickly:

Peter, I am more than happy with that, I myself was thinking 12, perhaps 20, strokes were needed and I didn't expect them to be worse than I received at school. So your suggestion is at the high end .You can leave the spanking to me, I don't particularly want another man's hands on her bottom again, and I will expect her to wear at least a thong, she should be thrashed on the bare, but you don't need to see everything. A little modesty is needed.

If this is OK with you, noon on Saturday would be fine, if that's not too early for you.

Here is the address. It shouldn't be hard to find.

Regards

Roger Pendleton

I immediately copied the reply to Angela, with a note, 'So is this OK, young lady?'

The response was just as quick, 'Yes, sir, reluctantly. I guess that's as good as it gets. Well done, don't let me down.'

I found the picture she had send me, printed it up on A4 paper and pinned it to my board in the office. She was a stunner, a real yummy mummy. Saturday couldn't come soon enough.

I was awake by 6.00 a.m. on the Saturday, I knew I wouldn't get to sleep again, so I got up and slipped out to the gym – an early morning spinning class and a swim would get me in shape. I dressed in my best suit; a fair old splash of Paco Rabanne and a spot of breakfast and I was ready for the off.

'You look as if you're up to no good today,' one of my friends at the gym said. I smiled at him, if he only knew the truth.

I was on the North Circular before long, my canes in a

cardboard tube in the boot, and within half an hour I was on the A12 heading out for Chelmsford and the countryside beyond.

I arrived in their village 40 minutes early, located the house, which was an enormous eight- to ten-bedroom pile with a Jag on the drive plus a Discovery and a couple of run-arounds. These people were seriously well-heeled. I dropped into the village pub and had a coffee. As the time reached ten to twelve, I headed back up the street and pulled up on their drive. I walked across the gravel and rang the bell, it was Angela herself who answered, looking as if she was just back from the gym, or as it turned out, a run, tight pants and a running vest that left her midriff bare. She was more stunning even than her photos had suggested, she winked at me, 'Roger, it's for you,' she called down the hall.

He came to the door 6' 4", perhaps even taller, rugged and handsome – even I could see that. Why on earth had she been playing around with him at home?

'Come in, I want you to meet my wife, Angela. Though I think you know each other already, don't you?' Angela looked surprised, she was a good actress.

'I don't think so,' she replied, 'where do I know you from?'

'He's Peter Jones,' the husband countered, 'who has always wanted to cane you. You, even in your sordid little world, have always declined; today I thought I would give him the opportunity.' She gaped at him.

'You have been insisting for weeks that I need to find a different method to punish you, other than leaving you. Mr Jones is it, let's see if you enjoy it as much as you do in your sordid fantasies.'

Roger was clearly getting angry, which was making Angela nervous too, time for me to take control.

'Mrs Pendleton,' I announced, 'I am indeed that man, and I am indeed about to give you the caning that you so richly deserve. I don't know what you have been doing to your husband but from what he says I am amazed he is still here.'

To my surprise Angela burst into tears, real ones, 'But you can't do that,' she sobbed, 'it's against the law, if you come near me I'll call the police!' She was putting on a good show, and so was I.

'I appreciate that, Mrs Pendleton,' I continued, 'your husband wants me to give you 24 strokes of the cane, after he has spanked you. Whether you want me to follow his wishes is entirely up to you, you are aware of my reputation, the next half hour is going to be very painful if you decide that I should stay, but you will live to tell the tale; you know that. I know you have spoken with others I have caned in the past.'

She was still sobbing. 'But, sir,' she was getting into the act now, starting to use the code we had discussed behind Roger's back – 'sir' to continue, 'Peter' to stop – 'this was only ever a fantasy for me, it's not something I can do and my husband knows that.'

I looked at Roger, 'I hope you haven't been wasting my time, it was a long drive here.'

'I don't think so,' he came back to me, 'I know it's my wife's call and, if she chooses to send you away and not accept the punishment, then I will give you £500 to cover your expenses as promised.' This was news to me – we had never discussed money, '...but, Angela dear, you need to understand how much you have hurt me, I'm willing to make a go of it for the kids' sake, but you have to take some pain too, real pain. It's your decision, but if you tell Mr Jones to leave, then I shall leave you, file for divorce, take the kids with me and your pornographic photo collection will be with Social Services on Monday morning.

This chap was for real and quite scary, I was glad Angela was in on the plot, or I don't think I could have stayed much longer.

We were sitting in a hallway so large that it was practically a small lounge, with sofas and a TV. 'Angela, go and make Mr Jones a pot of coffee and take it to the dining room,' Roger said. She left for the kitchen and he went up the stairs leaving me alone. Five minutes later, she returned, ready to usher me into the dining room. She whispered, as we walked down the passage, 'Please don't hold back, that will only anger him, but please get it over with quickly.'

I wasn't at all sure that I was going to obey the second of those instructions: not my style, dear reader. The dining room was large with a small ante-room attached, on the table were a pot of coffee and a fairly serious-looking cane, probably a little thicker and longer than my own, I was going to have to be careful here not to really hurt her.

Her leggings had gone only to be replaced by a dainty pair of white tennis shorts that accentuated her long legs beautifully; she was a real athlete. I found out later that she ran marathons.

I sat down and she poured me coffee. Roger came

back in and said 'If you will excuse me, Mr Jones, I am going to take Angela next door, I have my own business to deal with first.'

She followed him out and the door closed, I couldn't quite hear what they were saying, but two minutes later the first smack rang out and then the second and the third, it went on until I had long since lost count. I heard her moaning and then at first sobbing quite gently but eventually she lost control and was sobbing loudly, which didn't stop him, it went on for a full two minutes longer. I had a strong erection by the time he had finished, most embarrassing, but at least she wasn't going to have to go over my knee and detect it! I had a specific job to do and I somehow knew that for her own good I shouldn't spare the rod too much.

The spanking stopped and a minute or two later so did the sobbing, I stood up and flexed the cane, it was very flexible indeed for its thickness – it would sting and thud in fairly equal measure, I imagined.

A few minutes later there was a knock on the door, 'Come in,' I said, rather startled. Roger followed her through the door, towering over her.

'My wife is ready for you now, Mr Jones,' he announced.

'Stand up straight then, girl,' I countered, 'and put your hands on your head and look at me when I am talking to you. You know why I'm here, don't you? You are a cheat and an adulteress, your husband has been magnanimous enough to agree to forgive you, if you agree to being suitably punished.'

'Yes, sir,' she responded, 'I am so grateful for that.'

'And you understand the punishment will be 24 strokes with this cane?'

'Yes, sir.' She looked genuinely terrified.

'You may stop me at any time but, if you do, your husband may not keep to his side of the bargain either. Is that clearly understood?' She nodded. I looked her straight in the eye and asked, 'Are you ready for this, young lady? You do realise you won't be able to sit down for a week once I have finished?'

'I don't think I could sit down now, sir!' she replied, showing her spirit. 'Please, sir, can we get started?' she asked.

'When your husband is ready,' came my reply, ceding a little control to him. 'Shall I do it?' I looked at him.

'Yes. Go ahead. Give the bitch what she deserves,' he rasped. I still wasn't quite sure about his anger levels but I hoped this was cathartic and that he was getting it all out of his system, once and for all.

'We will have six with your shorts on first then, young lady, and then see where we go from there. Touch your toes!' No need to ask if she could do it – she was lithe and athletic, although she was now sweating ever so gently.

As her shorts rode up, I could see French knickers and, more shockingly, the reddest, sorest angry-looking arse I had ever seen, Roger had certainly done a thorough job on her, she was definitely warmed up.

I raised the cane. 'Count them for me, Mr Pendleton.'

'One,' he said a few moments later and rather too loudly. Swish went the cane as it arced through the air, biting into her buttocks and causing her to cry out in pain. I had started with a heavy stroke, I wanted the husband to feel sorry for her, not to be egging me on to go harder. He seemed rather taken aback by the ferocity of it; good, I thought. We stood there for a good minute, Angela didn't move a muscle, brave girl, I thought.

'When you are ready, Mr Pendleton,' I said, thinking he had forgotten we were waiting for his call.

He clearly had, he hastily called out 'two'. The cane arced towards the shorts-clad bottom again, a ten second delay and a further yelp – only a yelp this time, I had been much more gentle.

'Three,' from Roger fairly quickly. The cane sliced the air again, this time catching her bare flesh at the top of her thighs just below where her shorts started. A red line quickly formed where the initial white stroke had been laid. I felt the burn for the poor girl. 'Four.' Thhwackkkkkkk. 'Five.' Thwackkkk. 'Six.' Thwackkk. She was bawling already. I really didn't think she was ready for this. 'Stand up!' I ordered, she got to her feet, sobbing her heart out, tears running down her cheeks, 'Are you two both sure you want me to continue?' I looked at both of them in turn, Roger had started to look uneasy, but wasn't ready for me to stop quite yet and Angela knew it. I had to wonder where consent started and finished!

I let her rest for a good five minutes, but she soon seemed willing to continue, it was about getting it over with. I needed to stop being such a bastard and get it done with.

I reached forward, put my hands in the band of her shorts and flicked them down. She was wearing French knickers which covered her quite well and underneath was a tiny pair of panties, hardly bigger than a thong. Two pairs of knickers, well! I thought, that would have earned you extra strokes in my day.

'Touch your toes again.' She quickly got into position and the shorts fell to her ankles. I took the hem of her panties and pulled them up, baring as much flesh as I could.

I stepped back and swung again: a sharp crack but with no real effort in it. I really needed to go gently on her, five more times I followed suit, the whole thing was over in twenty seconds. I was trying to make life a bit easier for her, too easy perhaps. Roger certainly thought so. He called me into the side room, 'For her sake,' he barked, 'you need to put some effort in. We agreed this was for real not pretend, if I am to keep my end of the bargain you need to keep yours.' I was ready to argue with him, but I realised that he was right and that, anyway, she didn't want me to go easy.

We returned to the dining room, Angela was rubbing her bottom looking quite composed again now, all things considered. 'Right then, time for the knickers to come down, let's get this job finished.' She stepped out of her lacy knickers, leaving only the tiny briefs. 'I said off, young lady.'

'She looked at me, 'Roger said I was to wear a thong, sir.'

'That's not a thong – OFF!' I ordered, wondering if Roger would argue, knowing that this moment was at the heart of Angela's fantasies. He didn't argue; in fact he seemed almost struck dumb. She was enjoying it.

'Bend over the table, Angela, and, Roger, please take her hands, make absolutely certain she stays in position.' He moved to the opposite side and stood at her head taking her wrists firmly and pinning her to the desk.

He didn't have the view I had of her perfect bottom, bright red and already covered with fairly angry weals. Her shaven quim was parted and clearly moist, I longed to touch it, but knew it was out of bounds.

I eased her feet apart, spreading her cheeks wide, and her lips parted further, too – it was difficult to distinguish which was the pinker and more vivid.

'This time I will count to twelve, young lady.' I waited ten seconds. 'One.' I raised the cane and laid it harder on her than I had ever laid a cane stroke on anyone before; I needed to know what they would be satisfied with. She screamed, her body bucked, but Roger held her firmly in place.

'Two.' Same again, this time I was a little low and the cane burned into her thighs – ouch! I felt really sorry for her; she was straining to get up, but Roger held her firmly, although he was again starting to look concerned. The first weal had already changed from red to purple.

'Three.' I aimed again, just as hard and right into the sweet spot between buttock and thigh; this time it went purple almost before it went red. Tears were pouring from her eyes and Roger was using a lot of strength to keep her pinned to the table.

'Are you ready for more, young lady?'

'Yes, sir,' she responded, giving me the code word to continue, I hadn't broken her yet.

'Four.' The cane lashed just half an inch above the last stroke, and she really screamed. Roger was looking more than uneasy.

I looked up at him, towering over me. 'Is this to your satisfaction, Roger, or do I need to put some more effort into the last six?' He kept silent – a little embarrassed now, perhaps.

'Five.' Another perfect stroke an inch above the last and completely parallel, Angela was screaming so loud that I wasn't sure if it was genuine or acting. I checked again if she wanted to use the safe word, 'Ready, Angela?'

'Yes, sir.' The cane flew into her thighs again, whipping though the air.

'Six.' The stroke landed right on top of the earlier stroke to the sweet spot; she cried and cried and cried almost uncontrollably. I still didn't think she had had enough, but Roger certainly had. He loosed his grip on her arms; walking round the table he picked her up and took her in his arms. 'I think she's had enough, Peter, I did say from the off eighteen was sufficient, I hope you agree I am right.'

Looking again at her angry buttocks and thighs, I was sure he was. What had I done? Why had I allowed Roger to push me into hurting her so much? However, then I thought, had she secretly enjoyed it?

Roger laid her on her stomach on the sofa, and started to rub her bottom with Arnica cream. Soothing away her troubles.

I knew I was rapidly becoming unnecessary. Roger poured another cup of coffee, but I refused. 'Time I wasn't here,' I suggested, 'London beckons.'

Angela turned and looked up, 'Don't worry,' she smiled, 'that was fantastic, and I guess I ought to own up and tell you Roger was in on the secret too.'

I smiled and let myself out, in fact I smiled all the way back to Golders Green where I had agreed to meet my daughter for a drink.

GINNY

I HAVE OFTEN BEEN asked whether I believe corporal punishment can alter people's behaviour and lives for the better, I am also asked why many people of my generation have such an affection for the cane; these are two issues that I will perhaps attempt to address in this chapter, dear reader.

It's not unusual for a Spank Daddy to be approached by ladies looking to change their lives and break bad habits, it's normally about weight loss but it can be concerning anything from giving up smoking to overspending on credit cards.

For 95% or more of people the answer is yes, I can help, especially with the weight-loss issue. Of course a small number of people can't lose weight for medical reasons, but for the bulk of us it's simply about self-discipline, eating and drinking less, exercising more, and of course where self-discipline lets someone down a good mentor can step in and provide the structure and discipline to help change habits.

This kind of discipline is quite different to the 'sexy spanking' that most of us play for fun and enjoy. If you enjoy something and it turns you on, then the prospect of it won't deter you from bad behaviour, it will only make matters worse.

In these circumstances, then, I think back to school days, and school discipline. The description *benevolent dictator* spring to mind for the headmasters of those days. This was the person who set the rules for you, in general they were fair rules and you knew where you stood. As long as you chose not to infringe them, you could happily get on with your life; most people did, possibly with the odd detention or a few lines for late homework, but nothing too serious.

Unless, of course, one chose to break the rules that mattered. In which case you faced the cane, the ultimate symbol of the Head's authority. It was very important for everyone to be terrified of the prospect of the cane, so that everyone chose to behave and it was rarely used; as was the case at my own alma mater.

What was certain was that, if you did break the rules, there was no going back, no appeal, the Head's decision was final, bend over and experience a very painful lesson one would remember for the rest of ones life.

All this came to mind when Ginny first contacted me some three years ago. She was a chubby girl, not fat but chubby, she looked good but she had three stone to lose in order to look great.

In her late thirties, she had tried and failed for years to exercise any self-discipline. She was a single mum, with a daughter in her late teens, and wanted to get out, move on and rejoin the dating game, but she wasn't attracting the men she wanted, so guerrilla tactics were required. She lived very close to me and, as chance would have it, when we started chatting online we discovered that we were both members of the same gym.

This quickly led to us agreeing to meet for a work-out and coffee the following morning. When we met, I recognised her from some classes we had both taken; despite her baggy grey jogging bottoms, covering a rather too ample bottom, I had thought her attractive and had actually wondered why she hadn't made more of an effort to take care of herself.

I soon found out that her idea of a jog was no more than a gentle walk, she spent most of the time chatting rather than sweating. After an hour, I had covered three times the distance she had and was sweating profusely, she wasn't! So we headed for the coffee shop and sat down, both a little embarrassed by the fact that we vaguely 'knew each other', she went straight for the latte, but I stopped her, 'My treat,' I said, 'and it's black coffee.' She smiled and sat down.

She told me that she had been spanked in her youth but only by hand over her mother's knee. She felt that a spanking might be the way forward; she had always gone out of her way to avoid sessions with her mum, although she confessed that she did find the idea of being spanked by a man rather exciting.

'Well, that's not going to help then is it?' I smiled at her again, 'it sounds like it's going to have to be the cane for you, young lady.'

Her smile disappeared very quickly. 'I don't think –' she responded, 'I really don't think I could take that, it wasn't what I was thinking of at all.'

So I decided to outline my benevolent dictator theory. Like in my schooldays of old, we would have a set of rules, it would be the pub that was out of bounds, the gym that would be compulsory, with no truancy allowed. To back these rules up there needed to be the dictator, able to inflict something she was scared of, not something she rather liked the idea of trying, and, if I was to help, that would be the cane. I would be benevolent in that I would help her in every way to stick to the rules. I would train with her and work with her; she would perhaps get some spankings on the way to encourage her. But if she ever broke the key rules or lied to me, the dictator would take over, it would be the cane, no ifs, no buts, no maybes. Between six and twelve hard strokes, exactly as would have been given by a schoolmaster, no harder, no softer.

She said she needed time to think. I asked her why, and pointed out that she was not actually agreeing to be caned; that I was not going to cane her, unless she chose to break the rules she had set for herself.

I said that the choice was hers, and always would be, but I was asking if she was willing to submit to me, to let me run her life the way she wanted it to be, without taking any excuses.

'I guess you are right, sir,' she said very softly. 'When do we begin?'

'When will you be home on your own again for a couple of hours?' I asked.

'Tomorrow evening,' she replied.

'OK,' I said, 'give me your address and I'll be around at 7.00 p.m. If anything changes and you won't be alone, let me know.'

I was about five minutes late when I arrived the following evening, carrying my training bag. She let me in with a smile, 'What's the bag for?' she laughed, 'are you taking me out running?'

'No,' I winked conspiratorially, 'I needed it to disguise this.' I opened the bag and took out a senior cane, three feet in length and crook-handled. 'I imagine you haven't seen one of these before.'

'Buuttttt,' she was almost stammering, 'you told me that you had no plans to cane me!'

'Ah yes,' I replied, 'but I also told you that I would if you forced me to. This is just for you to keep hanging in your wardrobe, or in the bottom drawer; somewhere unseen where only you and I know where it is. Let it be a constant reminder of what happens to naughty girls! In twelve month's time when you've reached your target, it will be your choice to either throw it away or keep it as a reminder not to turn back to your old ways. Now, take me to you your bedroom, young lady,' I ordered, 'and show me where you're going to keep it.' I sat on the bed and watched as she opened her wardrobe and hung it where no one would see it, covered by a coat, 'And while you're at it, put these in your knickers drawer!'

I tossed her a pair of old-fashioned bottle-green gym knickers. 'Hopefully you won't need these either!' And with that I took her in my arms and we gave each other a huge hug. 'Are we going to do this then, young lady?'

'Yes, sir,' she replied.

I led her to the kitchen and inspected her fridge-freezer and store cupboard. 'No more junk food for you, young lady.' We rummaged through her kitchen together and threw away everything unhealthy. Once it had been binned and the remains of the booze had gone too, I opened a bottle of mineral water.

Her new life started there and then.

We talked rules, and this is what I laid down for her:

No junk food, but instead grilled meat, grilled fish and lots of fresh fruit and vegetables.

Gym minimum four to five hours each week – proper exercise. I would be there with her most days to help set her goals and make sure she achieved them.

No alcohol at any time or anywhere, without my express prior permission, which wouldn't be granted often.

'Is that all?' she said.

'What else did you expect?' I asked. 'Live like that and the weight will drop off you.' I pushed her shoulders back straight and stroked her bosom, feeling her nipples harden, 'And these will tone up! I'll make you the most desirable woman on the planet, not that you aren't close already!'

Then she led me back to the bedroom, pushed me onto the bed, deftly unzipped my trousers, and took out my now rock-hard cock.

'If you are going to work so hard for me,' she giggled, 'I guess I shall have to do something for you too.'

With that she took me in her mouth and expertly and gently sucked and nibbled until, some twenty minutes later, I came all over her face.

We cleaned each other up, and she showed me out of the house. '7-30 tomorrow morning then, young lady, and don't be late – we have work to do.'

We really had a good time over the next few weeks and the weight dropped from both of us, my wife couldn't understand why I was so keen on going to the gym all of a sudden but encouraged it anyway; she rather wanted a new me too!

Ginny had lost a stone in six weeks, and had got down to just over 11 stone, aiming for her ideal weight of around 9 stone. Nothing more happened between us sexually but I knew that it would only be a matter of time.

Eventually one evening when we were leaving the gym, she said 'My daughter's staying at her dad's on Friday, why don't you come over for supper? Surely I've done enough now to earn one of your sexy spankings?' she smiled. 'It's about time.'

I squeezed her bottom and replied, 'Of course, I thought you'd never ask!'

Our relationship was working out really well now, she was doing what I had asked of her and getting results, with little more than a few words of encouragement from me. We hadn't even talked about the cane since that first night, though I knew that she knew exactly where it was, and what it stood for, ready to be used at a moment's notice if she stepped out of line. But Friday was to be different, I planned to seduce her.

I wore my suit as I always do when meeting a girl to spank her. She was wearing tight white jeans and a white T-shirt which set off her blonde hair beautifully. She was so pleased to be in her jeans; apparently it had been five years since she had last managed to get them to fit. She was already starting to look really stunning and she still had a way to go to reach her target. We ate fairly slowly. Salad, fruit and a single bottle of wine between us, which was a real treat – neither of us had had a drink for more than six weeks. You will be impressed, no doubt, dear reader, with my devotion to Spank Daddy duty!

I helped her clear the table and then whispered in her ear, 'Come on then, young lady, let's show you what you have been missing.' I led her to the bedroom, and sat on the bed. 'Right, young lady,' I finally said sharply, 'over my knee.'

Down she went, and I started to slowly massage her bottom and then slapped it fairly gently. We continued like this for a good few minutes until she started to groan, my cock was erect and pressed against her stomach. I eventually pushed her off my lap and onto the bed, unzipped her and pulled her jeans to her knees, she reached for my fly. 'Not yet, young lady,' I chided, 'I haven't finished with you yet.' I stood up and tugged at her jeans, pulling them off completely, revealing a white lacy thong.

I pulled her T-shirt up over her head exposing her breasts, she wasn't wearing a bra. I quickly wrestled her back over my knee; although she didn't put up much resistance. When the spanking started again a few seconds later, it was harder and much more urgent: a dozen spanks and then a little rub, and then another dozen spanks. This went on for another ten minutes or so but now, instead of rubbing between spanks, I was entering her with one and then two fingers, working her into a state of frenzy, until she came.

I then made her stand up, pink and flushed, the thong came down and she was naked. 'Lie on your back on the bed,' I ordered, 'and tuck your chin up under your knees.' It sounded as if we were in the gym but this time she was naked and in the 'diaper position', as it's commonly known, showing me her all. I slipped a leather blindfold over her eyes and then took each wrist in turn, attaching leather cuffs which I clipped to the headboard. I left her there for a full ten minutes during which I undressed and composed myself. I entered her first with my tongue, playing with her gently until its tip found her clitoris, she quickly came again.

I picked up my tawse, around twelve inches long and two wide; she didn't even know I had it. 'Did I give you permission to come?' I asked.

'No,' she whispered, 'I didn't know I needed permission.'

'No what?' I responded, cracking the tawse hard against her already reddened buttocks.

'I am sorry,' she yelped.

'Sorry what?' I cracked it hard again.

She yelped again, 'Sorry, sir,' she responded, the penny finally dropping.

'Count to six, young lady.'

'One,' she responded.

'One what, young lady?' I cracked the tawse again.

'Er, one, sir.' She was close to tears now, straining against the cuffs, fully aware that I could see everything she had on offer.

After six strokes she was sobbing quietly but that

soon stopped when I slipped on a condom and entered her with my fully erect cock, gently at first, then with more urgency. I made her come again, and just managed to slow down enough to stop myself from coming. A little more urgency, another orgasm for her. I held myself still inside her until my need to orgasm had subsided and then started again, I think she had come five, perhaps six, times before it all became too much and I came myself.

I released the cuffs and took her in my arms, we lay there for a good hour entwined in each other's arms, until I realised she was asleep, at which point I extricated myself, got dressed and went home. When I woke the next morning there was a text for me that simply said thank you.

Spring passed to summer and the weight continued to drop off, she was only just over 9½ stone by the time she went on holiday in August, looking toned.

I had been spanking her and sleeping with her a couple of times a month, but she had a new boyfriend now. I couldn't complain, I was married and knew this all had to come to an end anyway once her goal was achieved. When she got back from holiday things weren't so good, though, she admitted she had been drinking every day, not every other day as I had allowed and she had put half a stone back on. I pulled my old headmaster trick, telling her first that she had broken the rules and I had no option but to cane her, but then relenting when she turned pale, and deciding to give her one last chance to get herself back on track. Gym six days a week and no alcohol for two months was the prescription, which should get her to target.

And my job would be done.

She had become close to the new boyfriend by now and her holiday weight came off quickly, but then we hit a plateau, a month went by and no more came off. So close and yet so far, with less than half a stone to go. We spent three or four sessions a week together at the gym but the invitations to 'dinner' had dried up, chatting one day we agreed we should do it one more time once she hit target, and after that we would go our separate ways. Although she had eventually confided in a close friend how she had lost the weight and apparently the friend was toying with the idea of calling me – Rosemary Conley had nothing on me!

Still the last of the weight wasn't coming off, however, and I didn't understand it. I questioned her one morning and asked her if she was sticking to the rules, as it was on trust, and reminded her of her fate if I ever found out that she was lying to me. She assured me she wasn't.

We had finished our regular Sunday morning session at the gym, a Pilates class which she did on her own and then an hour on the treadmills with me. She had weighed herself: still the same as last week. In fact she admitted she had put a pound on. We were sitting drinking coffee with a group of friends afterwards and Ginny was anxious to get away, which wasn't like her, she normally liked to chat on a Sunday morning, but she seemed ill at ease, and I was soon to find out why.

None of the others of course knew anything about what had been going on between us other than that as gym buddies we had both lost a lot of weight. Jane, her friend, was the one who spilt the beans, 'been working off your hangover, have you?' she asked Ginny. 'Good night in Shoreditch on Friday, wasn't it?'

I watched Ginny's face drop, we had discussed the hen night she had been going to on Friday and explicitly agreed she would not drink. No wonder she was putting weight on! Despite the fact that she was sitting almost next to me, I sent her a text, she jumped as the phone beeped and she read it 'we are going to deal with this immediately young lady' was all it said.

No longer was she rushing to leave, her conversation had dried up but she was still sitting there 40 minutes later, when her friend finally left the two of us on our own.

'I am sorry,' she blurted out a few moments later.

'You will be,' I responded, 'I am so disappointed in you, we've worked together on this for almost a year now, both sweated blood, and now at the last hurdle you have given up. What do you want me to do? Walk away and let you return to your old ways? I'm sure it won't take you long to put the whole three stone back on again.' I was genuinely quite angry but knew I had to calm down; one of the first rules is that you don't cane someone when you are angry. You need to be in complete control of yourself before you can be in control of her.

'Go home,' I ordered, I knew her daughter was at her father's for the day and the new boyfriend was away on business. 'I shall be there in thirty minutes and I think you know what's going to happen.'

When she opened the door to me I could tell she had been crying. 'Please, Peter,' she said, 'I really don't think I can go though with this.'

I looked at her with disdain, 'Well, that's always been your prerogative,' I pointed out, 'but if I walk out of the door with this unresolved this afternoon, then you won't see me again, find yourself a new sucker to help you while you ignore all his rules behind his back.' She burst into tears again.

As she lay sobbing on the bed in her tight navy leotard (the baggy grey joggers were long gone), I realised how far we had come and just how good her body now looked. Was she going to see it though? I felt sure that if she didn't she would return to her old ways.

'Pull yourself together, girl,' I admonished, 'you're not going to be the first to get a good hiding. I know you aren't going to be able to sit down for a day or two once I have finished with you. But you will live to tell the tale, and you will have shown that you have the strength to stick to your goals and the standards you have set for yourself.'

The sobbing stopped. 'I guess you are right, sir,' she said sitting upright. 'It's time I grew up, really, isn't it? Time I accepted responsibility for my actions.'

'I think so, young lady,' I said softly but firmly, 'now go and pull yourself together. Take a shower, dry off, put the gym knickers on and come into the lounge when you are ready.'

I sat back on the sofa and flicked on the TV as she disappeared to the bathroom. The EastEnders omnibus had just started, I got engrossed and then realised that she had been gone for nearly 45 minutes. I walked over and opened her bedroom door. She was sitting motionless on the edge of the bed staring into space, deep in thought, she was wearing a white T-shirt revealing the delicious shape of her pert and toned breasts, the gym kickers showed off her still tanned and taut thighs perfectly, in fact she had lost pretty much all the weight she needed to lose, but we both knew we still had this one last thing to do.

'Come with me, young lady,' I broke the silence, 'we need to deal with this once and for all, don't we? No point in hanging around.'

'No, sir,' she responded, getting to her feet and following me back to the lounge.

'Hands on your head,' I ordered. Her blonde shoulder-length hair was just about dry now, as she put her hands on it.

'We have come a long way together, young lady, and I am so disappointed that at this late stage you have turned into a liar. I am going to give you six strokes of the cane for lying to me and a further six for drinking on Friday against my direct instructions.'

'Do I go over your knee first, sir?' she smiled weakly, stepping towards me.

'No you don't, young lady, you're here to be punished not to enjoy yourself.' I had never caned anyone cold, without preparing for it, before, but I knew this had to be the first time. That was pretty much my side of the benevolent dictator contract.

'Are you serious, sir?'

'Yes,' I replied, 'fetch me the cane.' Ginny shuffled off with a look approaching horror on her face. She returned a few moments later clutching the cane.

'Does this really hurt, sir?' she questioned, 'it feels so light.'

'Ginny, my dear, this is going to hurt far more than anything you have ever experienced before, and you will feel so much better for it when it's over.'

I saw a tear run down her cheek again and decided it was time.

'TOUCH YOUR TOES!' She was well honed from Pilates now and succeeded in following my order with little difficulty.

I raised the cane and brought it swiftly down on her cotton-clad bottom, so much smaller and firmer that it had been at the beginning of the year. 'One,' I called as she let out her first yelp, 'two,' I called and unleashed the second, 'three,' as the cane swished noisily through the air and connected with its destination for the third time.

She made as if to rise, her fingers no longer touching her toes. 'TOUCH YOUR TOES, YOUNG LADY.' She abruptly returned to position and I let off strokes four, five and six in very rapid procession, she was on her feet and howling now, tears streaming down her face.

'I can't do this, sir,' she howled, 'please stop.'

'You can, young lady, and you will, bend over the table. NOW or I shall add two extra strokes.' She bent quickly over the table,

Seven, eight, swish, swish, she was almost screaming now; could I finish this?

I slipped my fingers into the elastic waistband of her knickers and dragged them down to her knees. 'Let's have a look, shall we?' I boomed. Eight vivid red lines criss-crossed her bottom, all very accurately placed – no wrap, nothing too high. In fact the first few were already turning purple.

I raised the cane again, nine, swish, ten, swish, this time I put a lot less effort into the strokes but aimed them perfectly across her upper thighs .The effect would be the same and she wouldn't be going to the gym for a while.

She still knew she had a safe word; would she use it?

The last two strokes were unleashed with unswerving power and accuracy into the sweet spot between buttocks and thigh, right on top of each other. I really thought we would disturb the neighbours!

'Stand up, Ginny,' I said quietly, taking her sobbing body in my arms, 'it's all over.' I knew it wouldn't be as the wave of burning pain from each stroke just grew and grew, as it would for the next few minutes.

I laid her gently on the bed, and took her tightly in my arms. Next thing I noticed was her hand inside my shorts, I still hadn't changed. My erection was immediate.

There was to be no foreplay, she was too aroused for that, this time she dragged my shorts off and climbed on my erection as I lay on my back, she very quickly brought both of us to orgasm. Had this been a 'sexy spanking' after all? I had tried so hard to avoid that.

'You really need to go,' she said a few minutes later, still sobbing, 'I need some time to myself.' I left her face down on the bed, her bottom and thighs a vivid patchwork of purple and red. I hoped she had learned her lesson, I hoped all this had worked, I hoped I hadn't gone too far.

I called her the following morning, she wasn't

going to work and was still rather sore, as she put it. She apologised once again for lying to me and promised me it would never happen again. It was a week before she called me and said she was ready for the gym again, but now the joggers were back, tighter and far better fitting but necessary to cover the marks, which remained for a further two weeks, the two on her thighs being the last to go. It was nearly December now, Christmas was coming – ten months since we embarked on our journey. We were both three stone lighter and I had more to go. She didn't: she looked stunning.

My phone rang on the first Monday in December, 'Dinner tonight?' she asked. I assumed this would be it, I was right, she proudly showed me the print out from the scales in the gym, 8 stone 10 pounds it said, and she looked fantastic.

'So I presume this is where I get my cane back,' I offered.

'No,' she replied, 'it stays where it is, I am certainly never ever going to put myself in the position where you or anyone else has to use it on me again, it was truly awful.' A small pause, then she smiled.

'But I would have never got where I am today without the threat of it hanging over me.'

With that she took me to her bedroom, no spanking this time, just orgasm after orgasm.

I have barely seen her since; she still goes to the gym but at different times to me and hasn't put an ounce of the weight back on again in the 15 months since she took her punishment. I hear she is getting married again soon, I wonder if that means I get my cane back?

So does it work? It would seem, yes, dear reader, with two provisos, the first is that you really have to want it to work, if you don't want to change, deep down, you won't. If, on the other hand, you want to change but self-discipline lets you down, guys like me are ready to help. The second is that you have to be prepared to face the consequences of your actions, however unpleasant they may be, but that's something we have all had to learn the hard way over the years.

CAROLINE

IT WAS A FRIDAY morning when I got the call; unusually it was a man's voice. As you can probably guess, dear reader, I was hoping that this wouldn't spell trouble, but he quickly introduced himself.

'It's Brian Forbes here, I believe you've been chatting to my wife, Caroline.'

The penny dropped straight away, I had been chatting on the internet to this lady for a while and she had told me that she only played with men her husband had vetted, and normally only in his presence too. She told me that he would be in touch when she was ready.

'I understand that you're quite a disciplinarian,' he said and then mentioned the name of someone who turned out to be a mutual friend, whom I had spanked rather hard a few months previously. 'She tells me you are very good and more importantly that you do not necessarily expect any sexual favours. Caroline enjoys being caned and I enjoy watching her – the deal is quite simple: we would like you to come around and spank her and then cane her, she will get aroused but you must leave quickly when you have finished, so we can enjoy ourselves afterwards.

'That's no problem, Brian,' I responded. 'You are sure, however, that this is something she wants and it's not just for your pleasure? I would rather like that to be confirmed by her.'

'I understand,' he replied 'but she does rather like the element of surprise, which is taken away if you want to chat first. I think you are aware from your conversations that she is serious.'

I thought quickly and decided that the safe word could solve the problem. 'Well, OK,' I continued, 'but she has to use my safe word, I don't operate without one. I have a simple system, as long as she is calling me *sir*, I take that as consent, as soon as she uses my real name that is the safe word and I stop. I hope you will explain that to her and allow me to do the same when I finally meet her.'

'That's fine,' he agreed, 'I can understand your concerns.'

I had never punished anyone in the presence of a man before, certainly not of a husband, but, from the photo I had seen, this was a beautiful young lady, in her early thirties, blonde hair and very fit: irresistible really.

I have always been game for a new experience!

'When did you have in mind?' I asked.

'Oh,' he replied, 'I was wondering if you might be free tomorrow afternoon, our daughter is going to a party, so we will have the house clear for the afternoon.'

I did have plans for the next day, but not ones that couldn't be changed.

'Of course,' I replied.

'Can you drop by at, say, 2.00 p.m.?' he continued, 'We have our own cane here that we would like you to use. I understand that you dress formally in a suit, which again is what she likes. She will be wearing school uniform, if that's OK with you.'

My jaw almost dropped to the floor, I was starting to wonder if this was real, but I knew that it was.

'I believe you have discussed some role-play scenarios with her online,' he said, 'would you please take the line that she has been caught truanting again, after several warnings, and now you are going to have to act.'

'That's no problem at all,' I replied, 'leave it to me. How many strokes of the cane does she need?' I asked. 'I find twelve is a good number, delivered hard enough to leave weals for a couple of days. Does that sound about right, or would she prefer more, but softer, strokes?'

'Oh, no,' he replied, 'this needs to feel like a proper punishment. Twelve strokes minimum, she has taken double that. But I am told you cane very hard so I imagine twelve will suffice, but please do not go softly on her in any way. I would like you to turn up at two promptly, as soon as the house is clear I shall tell her to put her school uniform on and tell her that you are on your way.

We chatted away some more, he gave me an address in a rather nice area of Belsize Park and he was gone.

Hmmm, this was going to be interesting!

Saturday dawned. I went to the gym and then swam

and showered before putting my suit on, unusual for a Saturday, and headed through the traffic towards Belsize Park. The house was imposing, no change out on a million pounds for sure, and there was a top of the range Mercedes outside; she had already told me she was a fairly high-powered lawyer in the city, so I wasn't surprised.

I rang the doorbell feeling quite nervous, wondering quite how this was going to pan out. He answered the door and immediately put me at ease, 'Mr Jones, I presume,' was his opening remark. 'Come inside.'

He wasn't tall, and was dressed casually in chinos and a polo shirt. As we shook hands, I wondered where Caroline was, but he quickly shouted up the stairs, 'You can come down now young lady, your Headmaster is here to see you.'

I was quite taken aback by the slim elegant young blonde who made her way down the stairs. Quite short, and dressed in a navy school skirt and blazer, white shirt, school tie and white socks to her knees. I guessed it was her school uniform and that she still fitted into it, to top it off her shoulder-length blonde hair was in a pony tail. I wondered if she had the navy knickers to match, but doubted it, she was from a different era. She did look genuinely nervous.

'So you are the unfortunate young lady,' I opened.

'Yes, sir,' she replied quietly.

'The safe word has been explained to you, hasn't it, young lady?'

'Yes, sir,' she responded. 'It is Peter, sir, I know that I have to call you by your Christian name, and you will stop, but I don't expect to use it, sir.'

'In that case, young lady, I suggest you go into the dining room and wait for me.' I already knew that Brian had placed the cane on the dining room table.

She disappeared through the door, and Brian closed it so we could talk. 'She's actually quite terrified to know that it's you. She's heard of your reputation,' he said. 'Though I know that this is what she wants and needs; I do discipline her myself on occasions, but never quite manage to inject the severity that she craves.'

'Shall we deal with her, then?' I said.

'Yes,' he said, 'let's do it.'

I followed him into the rather elegant dining room where she was seated at the table. She didn't move.

'Stand up, young lady, and show some respect!' I ordered.

'Yes, sir,' she responded and jumped to her feet, looking shocked, realising that it was really going to happen. Her skirt was too short, four or five inches above the knee, the skirt itself would have got her into trouble in my day, but of course I was delighted.

'Hands on your head, young lady, and look at me while I am talking to you!' I picked up the cane and stared her in the eye, while swishing it through the air menacingly. 'Twelve strokes of the cane, young lady, is the minimum punishment for persistent truancy.'

I thought she was going to burst into tears before we even started.

'I am really disappointed that I am having to do this. But you leave me with no option, do you, Miss Forbes?'

'No, sir,' she responded. Brian was sitting back in a chair and seemed transfixed by the scene opening up in front of him. I was warming to the occasion and so was my groin; pity I wasn't going to be joining in the after party.

'I presume you can touch your toes, young lady?'

'Yes, sir,' she answered meekly.

As you will know by now, dear reader, this is a question I always ask, but rarely do I get the answer I was looking for!

'Show me, then, young lady.'

She leant forward and touched her toes perfectly, the skirt riding even higher up and exposing her tanned thighs. I admired her posterior for perhaps 20 or 30 seconds, 'You can stand up now, young lady,' I continued, 'first you are going over my knee.'

I placed the cane back on the table, pulled a chair out into the middle of the room and sat down. 'Right then, young lady, over my knee.'

She bent forward over my lap and dropped onto it, she was trembling ever so slightly and I knew she would be able to feel my erection pressed against her flat taut stomach.

I grasped her tightly with my left hand to stop her moving and to pin her to my lap, just holding her in that position was such a pleasure. With my right hand I flicked up her skirt exposing her firm bottom which was encased in what could best be described as plain white cotton sensible panties. They were already damp! I slapped her hard on each buttock in turn and then pulled the panties tight up into her crotch to expose all the bare flesh I could. I then proceeded to spank her, six at a time, one cheek after the other, gently at first, but after five minutes her whole bottom was a bright shade of pink. Next I turned my attention to the backs of her thighs as Brian had asked me to.

'Am I getting my message through?' I chided her.

'Yes, sir, you are,' she responded.

I knew she was enjoying it. I slipped my right hand into the waistband of her panties and pulled them down to her knees. Her pink lips were parted and glistening, how lucky her husband was that he was soon going to be placing his cock there, when I had finished my task.

I rubbed her bottom for a few moments, briefly allowing my fingers to touch her outer lips, but without penetration; she gasped and moaned. 'Please, sir, more of that,' she cried. I knew it wasn't allowed, though, and so did she.

'Mr Forbes, can you pass me that hairbrush please?'

Brian stood up, even I could see the bulge in his pants as he walked over and picked up a large wooden hairbrush from the shelf. He passed it to me, 'Don't spare her,' he urged, 'she deserves every bit of this, and more.'

She gasped when the first stroke connected and cried out with the second, 'Get your legs apart,' I ordered, 'further!' She was displaying all she had and more as I laid into her soft cheeks with the back of the brush, within a minute the tears were flowing as Brian had assured me they must. As soon as they came I stopped and made her stand up, her knickers floating down round her ankles.

'Hands back on your head, young lady,' I commanded and she responded quickly, tears still gently rolling down her cheeks.

'I think she is ready for the cane now, don't you?' I looked at her husband, waiting for a signal if he thought I was treating her too harshly, none came, none was expected, really; we had discussed in advance what she needed and what she could take.

Was she going to be able to take the thrashing that was coming next, though? I wondered. Only time would tell.

'Touch your toes again, young lady.' The words were spoken very firmly and calmly. She bent over and immediately touched them with ease, her feet close together in the classic caning pose. Her panties still hung round her ankles and her rather too short navy skirt hung down her tanned thighs. With her knee-length white socks, she looked almost perfect.

'Can you raise her skirt for me?' I instructed her husband as we had prearranged. He stepped forward, lifted the hem and tucked it into the waistband of her panties. She was trembling again now, but only very gently, I could only imagine the butterflies in the pit of her stomach, and the stirrings no doubt going on below.

'Right now, young lady, keep very still,' I suggested quietly, 'if you don't and you move, the punishment will be increased, I hope you understand. I am sure twelve strokes of the cane will ensure you have second thoughts about ever missing school again, but if you want more you will get them.'

'No, sir,' she responded, 'twelve will be plenty, sir.'

'In that case, young lady, can I suggest you do not move, or you may find me starting all over again.' My instructions at this point were clear: cane her hard enough to ensure that she did in fact move, and that, I was advised, would probably involve bringing her back to tears. 'Are you ready, young lady?'

'Yes, sir,' she answered.

'One,' her husband barked, I lashed the cane hard and true and caught both buttocks perfectly, with no hint of wrap, thirty seconds later the welt was bright red.

'Two,' a second stroke, placed parallel to the first but half an inch lower. She gasped out loud but resolutely remained in position; she wouldn't much longer.

'Three,' the third stroke was quite deliberately aimed for the top of her thighs, she yelped very loudly on impact and within seconds was back on her feet, rubbing furiously, tears trickling down her cheeks again.

'Did I give your permission to stand up?' I asked.

'No, sir, you didn't but, sir, I couldn't help it.'

I looked to Brian, nothing.

'Miss Forbes,' I countered, 'bend over the table with your arms in front of you.'

She stretched her body across the length of the table, while her husband reached forward and brought each wrist towards him, tightly pinning her to the table. She wasn't moving now, and she wasn't going to be able to. 'Feet apart, young lady,' I added, 'as far as they will go.'

I spent some time making sure she was in exactly the right position with her bottom at just the right angle and her lips once more gaping before me, but this time I wasn't to touch, that was for Brian.

'One,' he started again, the stroke was far less intense this time, she winced slightly and strained to pull back, but her husband held her tightly. 'Two,' he ordered, more of the same, nothing like the power of the first three strokes, but enough to make her wince, she was meant to be enjoying it now: the delicious feeling coursing through her body. We took our time between strokes, with Brian calling the shots, but each time he left plenty of time for her to feel the full impact and aftermath of the stroke before the next landed. It was probably ten minutes later and about half an hour after I had first entered the house that he finally called twelve. She had been sobbing gently throughout that ten minute period, but now she knew it was finally over.

'Remain in position,' I ordered as her husband loosened his grip on her wrists. I stood back and admired my handiwork, three vicious welts that were turning an angry shade of purple and a dozen red ones crossed her perfect bottom.

I gently inserted two fingers deep into her crotch; she gasped out loud but I didn't keep them there long, though. 'I believe she is ready for you now, Brian,' I said.

He was already unbuckling his trousers as I let myself quietly out of the room, I stayed behind the door for a couple of minutes listening to her moans of pleasure as he entered her, before silently letting myself out of the house and heading for home. Job done!

NANCY

PERHAPS YOU HAVE HEARD it said, dear reader, that you're never too old for a sound spanking. Truer word was never spoken, in my opinion, and my opinion was reinforced when I first came across Nancy in a chat-room late one evening.

At first she was pretty cagey, asking all the standard questions and barely letting me get a word in edgeways. I told her all about my looks, my build and my experience, and we eventually got to the question of how old I was. I will confess to you, dear reader, that I have reached the ripe old age of 52, and a very well preserved 52, if I may so myself. I often lie about my age – increasing it, you may be surprised to hear. You see, it was only really when I turned (theoretically!) 50 that most of my lady internet contacts started to show any interest, even the younger girls, it seems, prefer an older Spank Daddy. I suppose it's just the way things are wired in the female brain. So I answered Nancy's question, this time being honest, '52,' I said, 'I hope that doesn't put you off.'

'Not at all,' came the response, 'you're not too young for me!'

'Why? How old are you, then,' I asked.

She seemed coy and wouldn't tell me, then she said, teasing me, 'Why don't I email you my picture and let you guess?'

I agreed, in fact I was rather enjoying her banter, and we exchanged email addresses. A few minutes later a picture of a very elegant blonde somewhere in her mid 50s, or perhaps late 50s dropped into my box. She had certainly been quite a looker in her day.

'Fifty-five,' I ventured.

'You're such a charmer,' came the response.

'Go on then, 58 absolutely maximum.'

'Let's just say I have had my bus pass for 5 years now.'

I did the arithmetic, 'No, 65? Never,' I replied, thinking she was winding me up.

'Sixty-six, actually,' came the response.

'Well, you could have fooled me. Sweet 66 and never been spanked,' I suggested.

'Oh no,' she replied, 'I have been spanked, before you were born!'

'Well, at your age, I imagine you're telling the truth, do tell!'

Now, dear reader, perhaps you're thinking that your favourite Spank Daddy must have been a bit desperate for a bottom to spank to carry on this conversation with an OAP. Far from it, I assure you, I had no shortage of willing female partners, but I was definitely intrigued by this lady. Also, while I suppose one shouldn't generalise too much, I have found in the course of my spanking career that the amount of fun I have seems to increase in line with the age of the lady I am playing with. Of course there have been some notable exceptions to this rule (two young ladies in their twenties come to mind!) but I was certainly not put off by Nancy's age, rather the reverse, in fact.

Forgive me, dear reader, if I take a little of your time to describe what this lady told me, but it interested me very much, giving me an insight into the world of domestic discipline in a time gone by. Also, I hope that, when this tale comes to its perhaps unexpected end, it will help you make your own judgement as to the wisdom, or otherwise, of my actions. I will précis what she told me, together with what I subsequently learnt when I met her.

Nancy was of quite aristocratic stock, being a very distant cousin of the Queen, she said, and had been born in Nairobi, Kenya, in 1940 just as war had broken out in Europe. From what she said it sounded to me as if her parents might well have been part of the notorious 'Happy Valley' set.

Her well-to-do parents never spanked her personally but her nanny had taken the hair-brush to her from an early age: often on the direct instructions of her father.

She had experienced her first caning at school at the age of 12, and her last at the age of 17. Returning to London in the early 1960s she had been very much part of the Kings Road set, eventually marrying an aristocrat with a penchant for spanking at the age of 26. He was 15 years her senior.

They settled into what the Americans would call a 'Head of Household' relationship, with a dominant patriarchal figure. They had four children, two boys and two girls, all of whom were regularly subjected to corporal punishment, both at home and at school. She thoroughly approved of this regime, and, while her husband often spanked her for fun as part of their sex life, he had also on occasion taken the cane to her, in exactly the same manner as he did to the children.

This was in the 1970s and neither she, nor anyone else in their social circle, it seemed, found any of this in the least strange or unusual.

Although at that time state schools were gradually phasing caning out, the upper-class with their offspring in public schools maintained the practice right to the bitter end in the mid 1980s. Even then, when he stopped punishing the children, he still continued to cane his wife for any serious indiscretions on her part, right up until his death eight years previously. Her last thrashing had been for flirting too much with one of his friends at a society ball.

Being so much younger than him, she had taken to finding lovers of her own age or younger and on occasion she had paid the price: accepting very painful canings that she didn't enjoy. The benefits of having a wealthy husband were not something she was going to give up in a hurry, so she had stuck with him long after being punished by him had induced any sexual arousal in her. She was now looking for someone to help her rekindle the fire, she said.

As you're aware, dear reader, corporal punishment has only become an important part of my life fairly recently, and the same is true of most of the ladies I had played with, so I was interested to know what its effect has been on somebody who grew up with it and lived with it. Of course a part of me thought this all sounded too incredible for words, but I was interested enough to offer her my phone number, I suggested she called me to chat, which is always the best way to weed out chat-room male fantasists pretending to be women!

(Although it has to be said that it's also occasionally an effective way of scaring off genuinely nice but timid ladies, by being too forward. It's a chance you have to take, sometimes, but I do particularly regret one extremely glamorous and quite well-known actress I scared away... but that's another story, dear reader, and I mustn't digress, must I? Anyway, perhaps I'll be able to win her round eventually and she can appear in volume two of my disgraceful memoirs!)

She came back again via the chat-room, however, and said that she would rather like to be spanked a few more times before it was too late. 'None of the email friends I have dared to ask,' she said, 'have been able to properly oblige me, they don't understand that I need more than a few gentle smacks, and unfortunately they never will. So I am here to seek the services of a professional, so to speak.'

So far, so reasonable, but then she continued, 'As well as that, my younger daughter, who has just turned 30, needs bringing back into line, she's far too wayward, and as far as I am concerned you are never too old for a good spanking!'

Despite my strong previous interest in the story, I thought, no! This is too much; it's clearly just a mad old man winding me up! Why had I fallen for it again?

'Let me tell you something,' I responded, 'I am only interested in consensual activity, which you know damn well, so stop winding me up, you sad old git.' Not, perhaps, quite as elegantly phrased as it could have been but sometimes one has to speak to people in the kind of language they understand. Anyhow, with that I closed down my browser and went to bed.

It was early the following evening, probably just after six, when an unfamiliar number rang through to my second mobile phone – the one I keep in the office, away from my wife, for the sole purpose of seducing potential spanking partners. I prefer not to reveal my main phone number until I know them and can trust them. Most of the women I encounter do exactly the same thing.

I picked it up and a very posh sounding lady answered, 'You're a very rude young man,' she said, 'you probably deserve a sound caning yourself.'

I had no idea who it was and quickly asked. 'It's Nancy, you fool,' she responded, 'you hung up on me last night, accusing me of being a man, remember?'

I was, for once in my life, totally speechless and could hardly stutter an apology. I had been so annoyed with myself for being, as I thought, strung along by an old pervert that I had convinced myself that there was not a chance in a million that the story was true.

'I think you ought to buy me dinner by way of apology,' she continued, 'I have a table booked for this evening if you would care to join me.'

Of course I was more than a little taken aback by her boldness; I was free and, almost, suitably dressed and more than a little intrigued by this woman already.

I arrived at her Knightsbridge apartment an hour later, a little earlier than anticipated, and rang the bell. A housekeeper answered the door and ushered me inside. A few moments later I was joined by a very petite, attractive blonde lady, looking even younger in the flesh than in her photo.

She smiled and looked up at me, 'You're taller than I imagined, Peter, and not too bad-looking,' she said, 'I like that. So, are you going to take me to dinner?' Her housekeeper came in with her coat which I took and held while she put it on. She really was little more than 5ft tall and terribly dainty, I couldn't imagine her being caned, the mind boggled.

I really was quite unsure about the whole situation. At the restaurant, she talked a lot about her life and we had reached the stage of coffee before I brought up the subject of corporal punishment, remarking that it was nice to meet someone old enough to have experienced the real thing. I didn't think that there were very many around, particularly ladies. And even fewer who had been using it in their homes right up until the late 80s.

'The early 90s actually,' she corrected, 'Anna was 15 the last time Daddy had cause to cane her, that would have been 1991.' Daddy! I thought.

'She lied to us,' Nancy said, 'and left us frantically worried for a whole night, having assured us that she was sleeping over at a girlfriend's house, when she had actually gone out with a much older boy and spent the rest of the night at his house. Daddy was so cross when she returned. She was punished then and needs punishing now.'

I paid the bill, we returned to my car and took the short drive back to her mews.

The housekeeper had gone home, and Nancy made a pot of coffee herself and brought it through with two cups. 'You look puzzled, Peter,' she said after I had poured the coffee and sat down.

'Well, I am a bit mystified,' I replied, 'if I understand correctly, you expect me to punish your 30-year-old daughter. That's really rather bizarre. I came here tonight because you intrigued me, and you still do, but I was quite serious last night when I said I only spank consensually.'

She looked steadily at me.

'And I think you will find it hard,' I continued, 'to find someone who will do it. I have better things to do than end up in prison.' I was really thinking it was time I left, but was still intrigued to hear what she was going to say next.

'Oh, it will be with her consent, I promise you, and you won't end up on an assault charge. She has it coming to her and I am sure she will accept it willingly, it's what she was brought up with, you see. It's what she needs and deserves to buck her up.'

I'm sure the incredulity showed on my face. 'And why on earth would she agree to it?' I asked, 'If she isn't into spanking and knows nothing about you wanting her to be spanked?'

'She's in trouble again, and I am the only person in the world ready and willing to bail her out. Yet again. And this time I am not going to do it unless she is prepared to take responsibility for her actions, I have already paid off her debts three times in the years since her Daddy died, he would never have stood for it. She's a spoiled brat and this will be the last time I bail her out. She lost her job again four months ago, she is deep in debt and about to have her home repossessed. She says she desperately needs £75,000 and thinks I am an easy target, that I will pay up before I see my granddaughter homeless.' She paused and looked at me for a reaction.

'But,' she continued, 'this time I have had enough. So, yes, I will bail her out but she has to be punished too and show some contrition for her actions, *before* I write the cheque out, so, Peter, I can assure you that she will consent.'

Did she really expect me to go through with her plan? I really started to think that she was unbalanced and I politely told her so. 'I am afraid, Nancy, that is not consensual in my, or anyone else's, book or in the eyes of the law. It may be with consent but only by virtue of you blackmailing her; your scheme could put us both in prison.'

'Please, Peter,' she replied, 'hear me out. She has been caned before as have I, I am not asking you to do anything to her that you won't have done to me first, I have not been behaving in a way that Daddy would have approved of, of late, and I am sure I would feel much better for it if you were to deal with me, as Anna will when you have dealt with her. We have in fact discussed it since my husband's death, and neither of us regret the treatment we received. Both of us, indeed all of my children, agree it was good for them, although only Anna knows that I had the same treatment from him too, that's our little secret.'

After this extraordinary speech, I decided that the time had come to put a stop to this. Whether or not what she was saying was true, which I doubted, I knew I could have no part of it.

'Nancy,' I said, 'it's been a pleasure meeting you. Really. But I'm afraid I have to go. I like to play, but I'm a lawyer, this is not for me. I'm sorry.' I left and went home, puzzled but very glad that I had, this time at least, been sensible.

I did wonder if I would hear from Nancy again. Although she was attractive, she was also trouble and, on balance, I hoped not. It was early on Thursday afternoon when another call from an unknown number came through on my second mobile.

'Peter Jones?' a female voice said.

'Yes?'

'This is Anna, Nancy's daughter.'

'Ah ... hello.'

'I have no wish to discuss family affairs with a stranger, Mr Jones, but –'

'Then don't,' I interrupted, 'I have no interest in your affairs, Anna, and absolutely no intention whatsoever of becoming involved in them.'

'I'm very relieved to hear it. My mother told me–'

I interrupted again, 'Whatever she told you about me, it's not true. I met your mother, she told me a tale that I didn't believe. It really is none of my business and now, if you'll excuse me, I must go.'

And that really was the end of it. In many ways of course it was one of the least satisfying of my spanking experiences, but it was also one of the most fascinating. The fact that the daughter had called me suggested that at least some of Nancy's tale was true. I had to draw the conclusion that being brought up with corporal punishment in the family wasn't necessarily a good thing!

Whether or not I upheld the honour and reputation of the Honourable Company of Spank Daddies, I leave it to you to judge.

At least the episode taught me a valuable lesson – which I'm duty bound to pass on to you, dear reader. Be careful. Be *very* careful!

ANTHEA

A SHORT STORY ABOUT one of my spankees' experiences with me appeared on one of the spanking sites on the web and aroused quite a bit of interest. Of course I was hoping it might bring me some new bottoms to spank, and, a couple of days later, an email dropped into my Facebook account, from a lady in Oxford called Anthea.

She told me how she had just read the story, understood that it was a true story, and very much wished she had been the girl in it.

I replied fairly curtly, 'Well, I guess you had better report to my office too, young lady, sounds as if you need to be caned as well.'

Minutes later, an email came back 'Would you really do that for me? I'm a bit flustered now. I never imagined you would suggest that.'

At this stage I had no idea who she was, how old she was, or where she lived, what she looked like or anything, her Facebook profile was completely blank.

I emailed her back again, 'If you're serious then I am, we need to discuss it in some depth first, but feel free to phone me.' I added my phone number; this was often the time that over-keen would-be spankees went very quiet and perhaps would suggest that we needed to discuss it on Yahoo for the next three months in order to 'get to know each other better'. But this time it was to be different!

I picked up the phone that was ringing on my desk and much to my surprise it was a very confident middle-class sounding lady. 'Hello,' she said, 'this is Anthea, but I am really not sure why I'm doing this!'

'I imagine it's because you need to be caned, young lady,' I responded, 'have you ever been caned or spanked before?'

'No,' she replied, 'I haven't but I have fantasised about it since I was at school. I passed my fiftieth birthday last week, and decided that if I didn't do something about it now, I never would. So here I am, hoping that you will help me.'

I was completely taken aback at the speed of events, but even so it was clear that this was a very sane, sensible lady who knew exactly what she wanted. She explained to me that she had been a widow for three years and had not had any kind of a relationship with a man in that time; she wanted to be spanked and then caned and she wanted to be caned hard, at least as hard as you got caned in schools back in her day. She wanted some marks to show for it, but was really unsure whether she would enjoy it or not, if she didn't, nothing would be lost, she would put it down to experience; if she did enjoy it, as she imagined she would, then she might want to do it again on an irregular basis, perhaps once or twice a year.

'When were you hoping this might happen, young lady?' I asked her. I was again expecting some prevarication, for her to suggest waiting a couple of weeks so that she could think it through properly first, but again I was surprised.

'Very soon, sir, if you can, before I lose my nerve.'

'Where do you live?' I asked. 'Do you want me to come over now?'

'No,' she replied, 'that's not possible. I am a vet and live above the surgery where I work; I couldn't possibly invite you here.' There was a pause and then she said 'I will have to come to your office, is tomorrow night convenient?'

'Yes, young lady, it certainly is. I will see you in my study, at 7.00 p.m. sharp, where I shall spank you and give you the cane. Is that understood?'

'Yes, sir,' she replied, 'fully. That's what I need. One last thing, though, sir, I want you to take all my clothes off, I haven't been naked in front of a man since my partner died, I would find it very humiliating and very much want that to be part of it.'

I loved this: a lady who knew exactly what she wanted, her fantasy, not mine, my job was just to act it out for her. She was also very clear that she wanted no direct sexual contact; I was ready to oblige, of course.

I told her to call me as she was setting out.

I sent her an email with my address setting out everything we had agreed quite formally, and asking her to confirm her consent in writing, which she did, just adding a brief note that she had butterflies already and had never felt so nervous, which was exactly what she wanted.

I thought the chances of her actually turning up the

next night were probably fairly small, although it was certainly far from impossible: she certainly sounded both keen and determined. So I dressed in my suit for work the following day, taking just that little bit more care, with a good squirt of cologne first. I made sure the office was spick and span, I had a gym class booked for 7.30 p.m. which I didn't bother to cancel, that would have been tempting fate too far!

Just after six, the phone rang; this time the voice wasn't quite so confident, 'Good evening, sir, this is Anthea, I am leaving now.'

'Good. I'm glad to hear it,' I responded, 'you're ready for the good hiding you so richly deserve?'

'As ready as I ever will be, sir,' she replied, 'I should be about an hour.' And the phone clicked dead.

Even for me the hour seemed to last for two; in fact it was nearly 7.15 and I was about to phone her to see if she had chickened out, when my phone rang. 'I am outside now, sir.'

'OK I'll come and fetch you.' I walked down the corridor and stairs to the street where I was confronted by a tall, slim, elegant brunette, getting out of a very new and very smart car. 'You're Anthea, I take it,' I smiled.

'And I presume you're Peter,' she smiled back weakly.

'Right then, young lady, you'd better follow me upstairs.'

Thirty seconds later we were in my office. I shut the door and asked her to take a seat. 'How are you feeling?' I asked.

'To be honest, I'm terrified,' she replied, 'I expected to be scared, wanted to be scared, but I didn't expect it to be like this!'

'OK, just take deep breaths. I'm not going to do anything you don't want me to, and you know you can stop me at any time, just by using my real name.'

'Yes, sir,' she responded, keen to get going. I, however, was still trying to make sure things weren't going too quickly and tried to calm it all down with some small talk; going into detail about what might happen, giving her some options, making absolutely sure she wanted to be naked. Never before, dear reader, had I been quite so meticulous about making absolutely sure that consent was actually there. I could tell it was though, really.

Eventually it was she who stopped the small talk. 'Sir,' she said, 'do you think we could get on with this before my courage completely deserts me? I really am very, very scared but I do want it to happen.'

'In that case, young lady, you had better get up and go and stand in the corner while I prepare myself.' I made her stand facing the door on which the cane was hanging on a coat hook. She had never even seen one before. I pulled the chair to the middle of the room and sat on it, a couple of minutes in the corner would be enough, I thought. I didn't want to lose her, and she was so, so nervous.

'Pass me the cane,' I ordered and she picked it up. 'In fact, hold it for a minute,' I said, 'feel it. You haven't seen one before, have you?'

'No, sir,' she replied, taking it in her hand, 'and it's so light, I can't believe it hurts that much!'

'You're going to find out in a minute, my dear,' I responded, 'but first you are going over my knee, give me the cane.' I took it from her, laid it on the desk behind me and sat down again. 'Right,' I said, looking her straight in the eye, 'it's time, over my knee.'

She leant forward and took up the position.

She was simply but elegantly dressed; almost as tall as me, she was wearing a dark-coloured dress which was set off with a single string of pearls and cream stockings. The stockings matched a suspender belt, I quickly found out as I ran my hand under her dress up her thigh towards her pert bottom. She certainly had the body of a much younger woman, though she had tiny breasts.

Her panties were soft and silky and just about covered everything, but the view was turning me on like never before. I rubbed her bottom for maybe half a minute and then slapped it; gently at first but quickly building into a rhythm; one buttock at a time, stopping and rubbing every twenty seconds or so. After two or three minutes, I pulled the panties down to her knees revealing her full moistness. I could tell that she was enjoying it thus far, she started to moan softly as the slaps got harder and harder, her cheeks turning bright pink.

I suddenly stopped and ordered her to stand up, I then told her to take her dress off, which she did, slipping it over her head and revealing a pink bra. She was such an apparently prim and proper lady that I had difficulty believing the vision now revealed.

She was quickly back over my knee, and the spanking started again – much harder, much more urgent this time, but the rubbing continued too. I ran my hand up and down each thigh in turn from knee to buttock, gently grasping her glowing cheeks between spanks. Why had I promised her no sex? I wondered, I wanted her so badly then, the first time that this had really happened to me. However I am always good to my word, what I had promised her was just a good caning and she was well warmed up now.

I told her to get back to her feet and to go back into the corner, now with her hands on her head. I moved quietly over, unhooked her bra and removed it. She was quite naked now, except for the necklace, stockings and suspenders, and they could stay, I decided, the effect was stunning.

I sat in my chair and lasciviously and quite deliberately eyed her body up and down; she quite clearly didn't know what to do with her eyes, one minute she was staring at me, the next at the floor. Clearly she was quite humiliated, clearly she was enjoying every moment of it.

'Right, young lady,' I looked straight into her eyes, 'twelve strokes of the cane, then I shall be finished with you and you can go.'

'Sorry, sir, did you say twelve? I was expecting six, sir.'

'I can't ever remember saying that, young lady.'

'You didn't, sir, but six is normal, sir.'

'It might have been at school, young lady, but not for a grown woman,' I responded. Was she about to safe-word me?

'Well, OK, sir, if you say so.' She looked most apprehensive, so I decided to press on quickly.

I picked up the cane. 'Bend over, young lady, and touch your toes.' She responded quickly, easily touching her toes – no mean feat for a woman of her age. The cane was the Junior, no Senior cane thrashing for this lady, but a pretty severe introduction to its junior cousin was what I had in mind.

'Count to six, young lady,' I said quietly, 'and stay in position until I have finished or I shall start again.'

'One.'

I started with a sharp biting flick, she didn't react other than to say two, and a second sharp flick was laid on alongside. She counted slowly but evenly to six, taking each stroke in its stride, very stoic. I told her to stand up and take a rest; she clearly still didn't know what to do or where to look, whether to run or whether to stay, but I did sense that she was terribly aroused and I was too. Were we both going to break? If she changed her mind I was ready and willing, and the bulge in my pants showed I was able.

I picked up the cane again. 'I will count this time, young lady, you just stay in place till I have finished.' The first stroke was much harder and a red weal quickly appeared. She winced, and I counted two, cracking the cane down simultaneously; she winced again but no sign of breaking down. I took my time, hoping she would stop touching her toes, hoping we could play the extra strokes game, but it wasn't to be, stoic to the last, she just winced even louder during the last two strokes, which I laid on very hard. Always save the best or worst till last.

I told her to stand up, with her hands back on her head, and looked at her near-naked body for the last time. 'Do you want me to rub some Arnica on your bottom?' I asked.

'Nooo!' She looked startled at the suggestion, 'I really must be on my way.'

'In that case, young lady, get dressed and you may go.'

Five minutes later she was gone, she had been in the office precisely 35 minutes, start to finish, only a day after the first email. I can't see that ever happening again, dear reader!

I phoned her in the morning to make sure she was OK. She had, she assured me, absolutely loved every moment from start to finish. It had been three times scarier and ten times more painful than she had expected, in fact she said she couldn't believe that anything could have been more painful, and more importantly she still could not believe what an enjoyable and arousing pain it was.

She hadn't expected me to rub her bottom and she admitted that it had got her so aroused that, when I suggested rubbing in the Arnica, she knew she would have succumbed to sex immediately if she had let me, and she really wasn't that sort of girl to go having sex with strangers in their offices.

My virtue in not taking advantage of her was rewarded, you will be pleased to know, dear reader, when she called me out of the blue a couple of months later and invited me over for dinner. We hadn't even made it from the kitchen to the dining room when she suggested showing me that her bottom had healed perfectly. Naturally I took a professional interest, she bent over the island unit in the middle of the kitchen and lifted up her skirt, revealing a distinct lack of knickers. I will leave you to imagine what followed …

SANDRA

THE FILM *SECRETARY* CERTAINLY raised awareness of the whole spanking /BDSM scene and it became the subject of polite conversation, both with business colleagues and dinner party guests. It certainly led to a couple of delightful encounters for me; Sandra had been my partner's PA for the best part of ten years, she was a charming, efficient, tasteful and elegant woman of 38, married with two children in their early teens.

I had the impression for a while that she was not exactly excited by her relationship with her husband, but was probably far too concerned for the children to consider leaving him. We probably went out for an after-work drink once a week, or once every two weeks at least, and we were good buddies. I had the feeling that either of us might have made a pass at the other, but ultimately we were both far too sensible to let that kind of relationship intrude into the office.

We popped into the local wine bar one Thursday evening to share a bottle of red and have a chat, her husband was away in Dubai on business and the au pair had agreed to look after the kids till nine, so we had a good hour to chat before she had to run home. I knew she had been to the cinema a couple of nights earlier with her girlfriend and it seemed a natural conversation opener to ask her what she had seen. She blushed every so slightly when she told me she had seen the film *Secretary*. I smiled back at her and laughingly suggested that I had never thought of her as that sort of girl, to which she answered 'chance would be a fine thing!' her face turning a marginally pinker shade as she spoke. All of a sudden, I knew that I had absolutely no option but to seize the moment. Not very sensible you may say, dear reader, and I must concede that you are right, but occasionally even a calculating bastard like me loses control!

'Well ... I have always thought we needed a little more discipline in the office; a sound spanking never did anyone any harm, now, did it?'

'Hmmm, do you think so?'

'I was caned at school and it never did me any harm,' I said firmly.

She was transfixed. 'Were you really?' she asked, 'that must have been awful. What exactly did they do to you? My mother always use to threaten me as a kid, and tell me tales of her visits to the headmistress, but she never did anything about it thankfully, though today I have to admit I sometimes wonder what it was really like.' The words poured out.

As I poured the second glass of wine, I was thinking that I couldn't believe how frank she was being, and knew it was time to be equally brave. I knew as a lawyer that this was no conversation to be having with a member of staff, but I simply couldn't resist it.

'Well, young lady, if you ever want to find out I am perfectly ready and willing to oblige.'

'Oh, sir,' she teased back, 'I would have never have thought that you were that kind of chap. But I guess you should never judge a book by its cover!'

'That's right,' I replied 'perhaps neither of us should.'

Suddenly the embarrassment of the moment evaporated, and we were chatting freely and openly, she was as bored with her sex life as I had been with mine of late and was keen to spice it up. She didn't want to get involved in a full-blown affair, but she was not at all averse to some fun, and this was something she really wanted to try.

'To be fair,' she added, 'I had quite an active sex life before we married.' She wanted some of that back again, with added spice.

I had to this point mostly steered clear of sex with spanking partners, but this was feeling like too good an opportunity to miss. She was a curvy girl, whose bottom was normally squeezed into a tight black skirt, it was never quite too short, but always threatened to be. In idle moments I had frequently mused as to whether she was a stockings and suspenders girl under her demure exterior, and it looked as if I might be about to find out!

I cleared my throat and went for it, 'I have done it before,' I explained, 'even in the office, occasionally, with girls I meet through the internet. In fact you may be surprised to learn that I do have a small collection of canes in a cupboard in my office – which is always locked – I have the only key.

She looked at me wide-eyed, clearly shocked by

this revelation. 'Oh my God! Are you serious?' I could see that she was now regarding me in a new light, her body language, with her hands resting lightly on her thighs, her shoulders back and breasts thrusting towards me, gave me confidence to press on.

'Yes, my dear, I am if you are, why don't you pop in to see me tomorrow after work and lets see what happens; there shouldn't be anyone around much after five. We could have a lot of fun together if we're careful.' She smiled at me encouragingly. 'You will have to trust me not to do anything harmful to you, painful perhaps, but the marks need not last more than a day or so, in fact in the early stages perhaps they won't need to last at all …' She still kept eye contact with me, '…let's take it gently, we can play it by ear, and see where it takes us. The game is quite simple, you should start calling me 'sir' any time the two of us are together in private. I in turn will call you young lady, or Mrs Ross. If at any time, any time at all, you are unhappy with the way things are going just call me Peter instead.' I paused to see how she would take it.

She sat back in her chair, steepled her fingers and said, 'That sounds sensible to me… Sir.' She laughed and touched my hand lightly. 'You may discover that I am not quite the lady you think I am – I may well produce some surprises of my own, too!'

'Don't you think I am surprised already, Sandy? I really can't quite believe we're having this conversation.' I spoke in my normal, conversational, voice. Then, to set the tone for what was to come, I looked at my watch and said in my best headmaster tones, 'Goodness, young lady, you're going to be late, I had better drop you home.' This was something I had often done before, she lived only a few minutes away in St Johns Wood. I dropped her off outside her rather smart apartment block, wondering if life was ever going to be quite the same again; we were going to have to be very careful to keep this secret. But all the same I drove home with a big smile on my face.

As I pulled up on my drive I heard a text message come in. I picked the phone up, it was from Sandy – *I am so excited sir* was all it said.

I picked the phone up and rang her. 'Mrs Ross, don't ever do that again!'

'What? Why?' she stammered, 'Why not?' sounding bemused.

'Don't you mean *why not sir,* Mrs. Ross?'

'Sorry, sir, yes, sir,' she replied, 'what is the problem?'

'My wife might have seen that text,' I replied 'and asked questions. So might your husband. We must be very careful – no text messages and no being seen together in public more than normal.'

'No, sir, you're right.'

'I know I am, Mrs Ross. I would like you to see me in my office after work tomorrow to discuss your behaviour further.'

'Yes, sir,' she responded. I clicked the phone dead before she could say any more and. immediately erased both the text and the call history.

Tomorrow would be an interesting day, I thought as I ate my steak and salad. I had another glass of wine and quickly fell asleep in front of the television. My wife roused me when she came in just after eleven, and we went to bed straight away. I was up for some fun, but as usual she fell asleep as soon as her head hit the pillow; still there was always tomorrow!

I was up at six and in my office as usual at seven knowing I had a long day ahead of me. We were just finalising a major deal and I knew that I would have an hour on the phone to Los Angeles that evening, ironing out the contract details. Perhaps Sandra could stand in the corner and watch me, I mused, we hadn't really discussed what was going to happen, which was unusual for me, but I knew I should take things slowly and gently, or it could end very messily. As usual I had no contact with Sandra all day, she worked in my partner's office next door; my own PA is very efficient and had all the documents I needed typed and ready for my negotiations just before five. She asked me if she could leave a few minutes early, I agreed and thanked her for a job well done.

I had no time to think about Sandy and what might happen next, as I buried myself in the documents one last time, making sure there were no errors. It was almost six when I had finished checking them. LA would be on the phone at any minute and I wondered if she had thought better of it, I was about to call through to the other office when the intercom buzzed, 'You wanted to see me, sir?' were the words I heard.

'Yes, Mrs Ross, please come through.'

The door opened and I saw Sandra slowly making her way through the door on her hands and knees, an envelope in her mouth, a direct copy of a scene from the film, and my eyes almost popped out!, I hadn't realised she was going to take it that seriously; I had thought I would have to lead the way.

She came right forward until she was under my desk and dropped the envelope at my feet. Neither of us said anything, just then my private line started to ring, it would be Bob Coombs from LA.

'Can you get up and stand in the corner, young lady, until I have finished this call?' I picked up the phone and quickly got into conversation with Bob, running through the finer points of the deal, then realised that she hadn't moved an inch. I pushed at her shoulder gently shooing her way, but she refused to budge. This was getting ridiculous; my crotch was already starting to bulge, but it jumped properly to attention, when she deftly unzipped it and grasped inside. Having loosened the belt on my Armani suit trousers, she quickly released my erection from the confines of my underpants and then very gently started tickling the circumcised head with the end of her tongue. The feeling was electric and concentration became impossible. I tried to push her off again, 'Can we save this till later?' I muttered under my breath, but she responded only by taking me deep into her mouth, bringing me quickly to the point of no return, but just short she stopped, releasing me for a couple of minutes. As you can imagine, it was one hell of an experience, but even so I was getting angry; I had worked on this American deal for months and I couldn't afford to blow it now. I put my hand over the receiver and said, 'Mrs Ross, get in the corner now, or you will live to regret it.' However, this only seemed to encourage her back into oral action, slowly taking me deep inside her mouth and slowly but surely bringing me back to the point of ejaculation. At that point I was simply unable to continue the call and had to hang up the phone. She must have heard it click because a few quicker moves had me spurting in her mouth within a few seconds. I couldn't believe what she had done, and had no idea whether to be pleased or angry.

She backed out from under the desk and stood up, her face and lips dripping with my come. She went and stood in the corner facing the wall, her hands behind her back without saying a word.

'I shall deal with you when I have finished!' I barked, I was sorry to sound so angry, when I had just had such a great time, but business is business. Without saying a word, I took my leather cuffs from my bottom drawer and walked over and attached them to her wrists, binding them together behind her back. That should keep her in place till I had finished, I thought.

'Turn round, Mrs Ross, and face me.' She obeyed, still fully dressed but with come slowly dripping down her face onto her pristine white shirt, the dampness serving to enhance her erect nipples: she clearly wasn't wearing a bra.

I picked up the phone and dialled the number for Los Angeles. 'Bob,' I exclaimed, 'where were we? Not sure how we got cut off there – was it your phone or mine?' It was 45 minutes before we finished our call, in all that time Sandra barely moved a muscle!

The deal was done. I felt elated, the occasion called for champagne and I intended to share a bottle with Sandra afterwards, but first there was more sexy fun to look forward to. Although I wasn't going to push her to the point where she would avoid any future encounters, this was far too special, I still had to be firm. After all she had just given me one of the best blow jobs of my whole life, I wanted more and the best way was to maintain a dominant position.

I looked at her angrily, though of course I wasn't really, I felt she would want me to keep up the pretence, 'You never told me that you were a complete whore, Sandra, you could have blown everything there.' She looked at me coolly. 'What were you thinking of? You know how important this deal is to the company!'

She did, of course, but she also knew that it was practically done before the phone call, and it wasn't really likely to get derailed at that late stage. She didn't say anything, though, but hung her head and looked out at me submissively from under her fringe.

I unlocked my cupboard, however, took out my senior cane, and swished it through the air. 'You haven't seen one of these before, have you, young lady?' She suddenly looked pale and hesitant, perhaps wondering if she had stepped in out of her depth; this was just where I wanted her, but of course without scaring her into safe-wording me.

'No, sir, but my mother has told me how painful it can be. Please don't cane me, sir!' There was a definite emphasis on the *sir*, so she was still up for it, but I had other ideas for that night – the cane could wait for later.

I quickly recalled my headmaster's words, 'Your mother was right, Mrs Ross, and I can assure you that if you ever pull a stunt like that again the punishment will be short sharp and extremely painful, far more painful than anything you have ever experienced!

'But today I have other plans for you.' I took a tissue and finally wiped the stickiness from her face, then I very gently tweaked her nipples through her blouse, bringing them to full erection. She had lovely solid breasts, neither too large nor too small.

I suddenly remembered that not only were her hands still cuffed behind her back but that my flies were undone, and in a few moments I stripped down to my boxers, hoping she would be impressed by my newly trim waistline, the product of many hours in the gym. Although of course I'm able to have sex with good-looking younger women because of the force of my personality, I retain enough vanity to want to be desired physically as well!

She was pretty healthy herself: size 14 I would have guessed. I slowly unbuttoned her blouse, releasing her fine breasts. I bent forward and took each nipple in turn into my mouth, squeezing it first between my lips before circling it with my tongue until she was moaning in ecstasy. Now it was her turn to be brought to a climax; when I had finished playing with her breasts, I pushed her forward across my desk and reached up under her skirt. She was a stockings and suspenders girl, and her miniscule white panties were dripping. I pushed them aside and entered her moist cunt with two fingers heading straight for her clitoris. Within a couple of minutes she shuddered and came noisily, thank God everyone had gone home!

'Did I give you permission to come, young lady?'

'I didn't realise I needed it, sir,'

'You need permission for everything when you're with me, young lady, you should know that. This is the second time tonight you have acted without permission.'

She looked at me, over her shoulder, slightly non-plussed, but she kept silent and made no attempt to move from the desk.

I undid her skirt at the back and let it fall to the floor, then pulled her knickers down and let them drift down to her ankles where she stepped out of them, still leaning over the desk, her bare bottom so inviting. Her black stockings were held up by a black suspender belt, she was wearing nothing else.

I went to my cupboard and took out my two-tailed tawse, and slapped it hard against the palm of my hand, so hard that it almost made me wince!

That made her straighten up so I took her shoulder and pushed her gently back over the desk, telling her to spread her legs, revealing her pussy in its full glory. I gently parted the lips with my fingers, I could feel her beginning to get excited again. 'The next time you act against my instructions or come without my permission I shall beat you hard, is that perfectly clear, Mrs Ross?' As I spoke I gave her one hard slap across he buttocks, which quickly turned bright red, she winced hard, her breath almost taken away by the force of the blow.

I then started to gently and methodically spank her, little taps so gentle but so rapid that I quickly lost count, her gasps became a little more rhythmic too, and every so often I would stop, and run my finger along her crack playing gently with anus and vagina together. I reached for my drawer, picked out a very thin vibrator, switched it on and very gently inserted it slowly into her anus. It was perhaps four inches inside her when she once again came shuddering to a climax.

Leaving the vibrator exactly where it was, I stood back and gave her another hard slap with the strap, and quickly followed with nine more, counting as I applied them rhythmically to her bottom, mentally counting 20 second intervals between strokes.

When she started to sob convulsively, I stopped and released the clasp holding her wrists together. She was red and she was sore, but she was clearly still highly excited, and so was I: my erection had returned with a vengeance, as I stood there in front of this beautiful, nearly naked, woman, naked myself except for my boxers.

She sank to her knees in front of me without prompting and pulled my boxers to my ankles. I stepped out of them, now completely naked myself. I grasped her hair tightly, and guided her lips towards my cock, controlling her completely, allowing her to nibble the head only to be pulled away again. Her tears had stopped as she attacked my member hungrily, clearly enjoying every moment of her task.

'Don't make me come,' I ordered, although I could feel myself ever closer to that ecstatic moment. I pulled her to her feet and took her in my arms and hugged and kissed her long and hard, noticing that her breathing was getting heavier again. So indeed was mine! I leant back against the desk and lifted her onto my cock to straddle me, her vaginal muscles gripped me tightly and five minutes later, I gave in. 'You may come, young lady,' I whispered in her ear as we both passed into seventh heaven. I hugged her tight afterwards, and she hugged me; it absolutely was some of the best sex I had ever experienced.

We both knew this wasn't just a one-off, that we were on a roller-coaster we had no means of stopping until it came to a stop of its own accord. We both felt a little light-headed as we dressed and headed to the nearby wine bar where our adventure had started only 24 hours before. This time the drink was Bollinger.

Life at the office certainly became more interesting after the revelation that Sandra was a spanko. Despite the fact that we had agreed that, unfortunately, she couldn't be spanked very hard or very often for fear of her husband seeing the marks, she did become very sexually submissive. Approximately twice a week the door would open after everyone else had gone home and in she would come, just wondering if there was anything she could do for me before she went home. I would simply reply 'of course' and she would be down under my desk unzipping my flies and taking me to seventh heaven with her exquisite blow-jobs; she was more skilled with her lips and tongue than any woman I had ever met, gentle one moment nibbling and biting the next.

Seeing that I also had a mistress at the gym who I was regularly sleeping with, my sex life had never been so active and varied, even if unfortunately none of it was with my wife. Was I ever going to interest her again? I didn't know. Was I that bothered at that point? No: if I could go on living with my best friend and our family while enjoying the delights of sex with two beautiful and much younger women, then wasn't I the luckiest man alive? And on top of that I had dozens of women on the social networking sites trying to pluck up the courage to meet me. Of course few did, but I was by now regularly managing a couple of random sessions a month and I was getting to the position where I could be much more choosy about whom I spanked.

I had always studiously avoided the clingy ones and the obvious nutters, but it equally needs to be said that, for me, it wasn't always purely about physical attraction; it was the ladies with deviant minds who I found really attractive, the ones with the most interesting fantasies that they wanted to act out.

I was having a lunchtime sandwich in our wine bar with Sandra when she mentioned how jealous her friend Pauline was: she was the friend who had been with her on the visit to the cinema that had launched us into our little affair. I had only met the woman once, she was quite attractive, although rather short and dumpy she had seemed good fun. Although she was a terrible gossip, by all accounts.

I was a little taken aback that Sandra had told her about us, doubting whether she would be able to keep the news to herself, and I told Sandra so, castigating her for not talking to me about it first. 'Did I give you permission to talk about us?' I asked.

Sandra could immediately see where this was going and whispered 'No, sir, I guess I didn't.' A pause. 'And I guess you're right, Pauline probably isn't the world's most discreet person!'

'You had better come to my office at the end of the day then and I will deal with you, young lady. Your husband's not back for a week is he? Then there are no excuses, really, are there? This time you have an appointment with my cane, I will drive you home afterwards.' She had gone very quiet.

'You can tell Pauline that I will deal with her as well at some point if she's really interested. Involving her is probably the best route to getting her to keep her mouth shut.'

Sandra had gone a little pale and said quietly, 'This is going to really hurt isn't it, sir?' I had to agree with her that it was.

'Yes I'm afraid it is, young lady, six of the best, and no sex whatsoever, you're going to find out what happens to really naughty girls tonight.'

She gulped, 'Oh dear, I am not really sure I am ready for this.' She sighed '… but I guess I do deserve it, and it is something I have wanted to try for years. I guess it's too late for doubts now.'

'It certainly is, young lady, and it's time we went back to work.' I emptied my glass and got up and we strolled back to the office together. We were back in work-colleague mode, but my mind was on what was to come. I wasn't going to beat her black and blue, but I wasn't planning to warm her up first either, it was to be a proper disciplinary caning.

It must have been nearly seven o'clock before my partner left the office that night, he stuck his head round the door, 'Sandra is still here, don't lock her in, she has a couple of things left to finish.' I assured him I wouldn't and off he went. The coast was clear.

I went back to my desk and hit the intercom button. 'I will see you now, young lady,' I barked, thirty seconds later there was a knock on the door. 'Come,' I said in my most headmasterly voice. She was about to get the full treatment.

'You know how much I hate gossip,' I admonished her, 'and here you are encouraging gossip about us. Don't you realise what trouble it would cause if this goes round the office or back into our homes? You can tell your friend Pauline all about your experience tonight and warn her that she faces the same if a word of this gets out.'

She looked at me steadily, but I thought I could detect a slight trembling in her hands. 'You can also invite her to join us at some point for some fun if that's what she really wants, but tonight isn't going to be fun, you are about to find out what real punishment is about – no warm ups, no games being played – just six very painful strokes of the cane. I very much hope I never have to do this to you again. I don't find it particularly enjoyable, but unfortunately it's necessary sometimes.'

She was definitely looking a bit pale now but I was getting into my stride. 'Hopefully, this experience will stay with you for ever, and as a result the next time you are about to open your mouth to say something stupid you will keep it firmly shut!'

Sandra now looked quite terrified, almost like a rabbit caught in the headlights, but she knew she only had to say 'No, Peter', and nothing would happen. But she also knew that she didn't want to, and I knew it too.

She was wearing black trousers and a white blouse, the office uniform really, some days a skirt, some days trousers, but always black and always with a white blouse. She was wearing a bra that day, and it would be staying on, this was going to be a very different experience for her. I had earlier taken the junior cane from my locked cupboard and hung it on the back of the door under my coat, I walked over to the door and locked it, just to be on the safe side, and moved my coat from one hook to the next so that Sandra could see the cane.

'Put your hands on your head,' I ordered. There was to be no corner time, but it did give me the opportunity to come up behind her, putting my arms firmly around her waist I undid the button on the trousers and hauled them down to her knees, she was wearing the tiniest of thongs; there was going to be no need this time to pull her panties down for what I had in mind.

I stood back and admired her briefly.

'Touch your toes!' She bent forward without a struggle in her flat-heeled shoes, and touched the tip of her toes with her fingertips, her feet firmly together in the classic pose.

'This will be a six word lecture, young lady.'

'I...' The cane hissed through the air biting into her buttock, she gasped as the pain seared through her bottom.

'Will...' A second red line appeared .

I waited thirty seconds, she was trembling and clearly finding it difficult to maintain her position.

'Be...' I barked out the word and launched the cane arcing through the air for the third time. She started to sob.

'Far...' whack, 'more...' whack, 'discreet' whack. Ten seconds later it was all over and she was howling with pain, tears pouring down her cheek.

'Get dressed,' I ordered, and she quickly retrieved

her trousers and put them back on. It took her some ten minutes to compose herself while I sat in silence. 'I hope you have learned your lesson Mrs Ross,' I broke the silence which previously had only been interrupted by her sobbing.

'Yes, sir,' she replied quietly, 'I won't do it again.'

'Then let's go.' I opened the door and, locking up as I left, led her from the building. She winced audibly when she sat in the car seat. 'I think you are going to be very tender for a day or so,' I suggested, 'I am sorry about that but it was necessary.'

'Yes, sir, I know.'

When we pulled up outside her apartment I leapt out and opened the door for her, and offered her my hand to get out. I had an erection and although I knew her flat was empty, I did nothing other than sit and watch as she let herself into the house.

Of course I did wonder whether I had pushed her too far this time, but she seemed happy, and after all she had told me several weeks previously that she harboured a desire to be properly caned. I wondered if, come the morning, she would harbour the desire to do it again.

I got home, poured myself a large malt whisky and was soon in bed asleep. I didn't even hear my wife come in and the following morning I was up at six and was in the gym long before she woke up. That had been the pattern of our lives of late, we slept in the same bed, but were rarely both awake at the same time. I was beginning to suspect that she was having an affair too, but with everything else going on in my life, I wasn't sure that it bothered me.

LUCY

I HAD BEEN FASCINATED, right from my early days of chatting to girls online, as to how many were into the so-called 'school scene', where you would get a small group of 'pupils' turn up at a 'school room' somewhere and spend the evening, or perhaps even the whole day, doing 'real lessons' with 'real punishments' from the old days. I even saw a place in Herefordshire where someone ran a 'boarding school' that you could attend for the weekend. As I say, it fascinated me but it was never something I rushed out to try; in general I am much more of a private person, preferring one-on-one encounters, but I imagine you know that already!

I had met Lucy briefly in a chat room and we had quite quickly hit it off, at least at the friends level, and we were soon chatting on the phone and emailing each other on a regular basis.

My interest really rose after a few weeks, however, when she admitted to me that she was a serving policeman, a sergeant no less, dear reader, and once I had access to her vanilla Facebook page there was no question but that she was telling the truth. Equally I had no doubt, from other photos she sent me, that she enjoyed nothing more than dressing up in her old school uniform for six of the best, apparently without warm-up spankings. She liked it cold and real, it seemed. Her regular Dom was an older colleague at work, quite how they had got together in the first place she had never been willing to explain. She was in her early thirties, she was married and, as usual, her husband knew nothing. She only managed to get disciplined a handful of times a year, based around his business schedule.

She was happy with what she had, but somehow felt her sessions lacked authenticity and a degree of strictness. She frequently challenged me to come up with a scenario for her that was real – absolutely real with no hint of play about it.

At the same time as this was going on, my meetings with Simone and Andrea, after my inspections of their flat, would often end up with chats about the real thing, what was it like, what Mum had been through in her youth, etc,. They were absolutely fascinated, and, despite my warnings that cold caning was a particularly unpleasant experience (from what I knew and had been told), they too were both keen to give it a try, if only to say they had 'got the T-Shirt'. They had got the tidiness habit by now and it was clear that my inspections weren't, unfortunately, going to enable me to use the cane hanging on their bedroom door.

I guess it was a desire I understood and I racked my brains for a while as to how their wishes might be granted. Lucy had made it very clear that what she was looking for was an authentic session, preferably with one or two other girls, but definitely not as part of a public party, she couldn't consider public exposure given her profession and also she needed to feel safe and comfortable with the people she was playing with.

I told her about Simone and Andrea, also telling them about her, and they were keen to meet, which they did a couple of weeks later, in a City wine bar.

It was just the three of them, without me, and apparently they enjoyed a fairly riotous evening, though the two younger girls both agreed that Lucy was pretty scary herself in her policeman mode, and said they found it hard to believe she was really a sub.

Later the same week I met Lucy in the flesh for the first time for a quick drink in El Vino's, near Blackfriars Bridge, we quickly hit it off too and our plot was hatched. I had been aware for some time of a 'dungeon' in East London which had an authentic Headmaster's Study attached to it, apparently it had been fastidiously decorated to recreate the feel of a 1960s schoolmaster's office. Even the books were from the era, nothing had been left to chance.

I rang and booked it for a two-hour session on the Monday evening of the following week. Lucy's mind was as deviant as mine and we had hatched up a plot that I knew the girls would enjoy, or at least it would give them the experience they craved; only time would tell whether they would enjoy it or not.

Lucy's school uniform was maroon in colour; I dropped by the girls' flat on the Friday evening, leaving an envelope containing money and a picture of Lucy in her uniform, with instructions to buy something over the weekend as close to matching as was possible. I told them to be home from work by six on Monday, to dress in their uniform and to await further instructions. They were to make no further contact with me in the meantime.

Andrea texted Lucy later that same evening to see if she knew what was going on, Lucy lied and texted back saying no she hadn't got a clue. In fact Lucy knew everything and was an integral part of the plot.

It was a warm spring day on the following Monday as I headed along the Embankment in the early evening. People were sitting drinking outside the bars, probably for the first time that year, certainly the first time I had seen them in any numbers. As I drew under Blackfriars Bridge, I spotted a policewoman in uniform by a bus shelter with a holdall slung over her shoulder. I pulled over and opened the door so that she could hop in, as I looked at her I could see Lucy was primed and ready for action. It took us about twenty minutes to make our way to the girls' flat, boy were they in for a surprise!

I sat in the car across the street from the flat watching as Lucy knocked on the door. Andrea's head appeared around the door, clearly expecting me, and she looked surprised as Lucy pushed the door open, revealing Andrea in a maroon skirt and sweater. It looked to me as if it took a good thirty seconds of animated conversation before the penny dropped and she realised it was Lucy she was talking to.

They both went into the house and shut the door, I could only imagine the scene inside, with Lucy lecturing the two younger girls as to how there was no point in arguing, the local shopkeeper had clearly identified them as shoplifters, and how she knew very well from the uniform they were wearing that they had a headmaster who took a very dim view of girls who brought the school into disrepute. She was there to arrest them on the spot if need be, though the shopkeeper had suggested to her that she might not press charges if the girls allowed the Headmaster to deal with the matter. She would be saying that she felt confident that he would treat them firmly and fairly and leave them with no more than a sore bottom rather than a criminal record. She was prepared to go along with that provided that they were happy to be escorted to the school immediately, where the head was waiting to deal with them.

Five minutes later the three of them emerged, the two younger girls' overcoats covering their uniforms, with Lucy leading the way. She opened the back door and ushered them in before climbing into the passenger seat beside me.

We drove in silence for 15 minutes until I pulled up in front of our destination. I parked the car and turned to Lucy, 'Give me ten minutes and then bring the girls up.'

I got out of the car and went into the building, taking Lucy's hold-all with me, she would soon be needing it!

I had done a reconnaissance of the place earlier in the day and paid the owner cash in advance. I'd checked out the facilities, the dungeon room was quite an eye-opener, but that was for another day, perhaps, tonight we were in authentic schooldays mode.

The study was a largish room, probably around 20 feet square, with a leather-backed chair and an old oak desk, ancient photos of previous headmasters hung from the wall, and lying on the desk was a leather bound volume marked *Punishment Book.*

On the wall was a rack holding no fewer than twelve canes. They were of ascending size, the biggest, a real brute, on top; each one rested horizontally between the two uprights.

I started to think that I was going to enjoy my evening!

What looked like a genuine Lochgelly tawse hung underneath the menacing array of canes. I had never seen or used one before and was almost tempted to try it, but reflected that it would be best kept for another day. Hanging on the back of the door was the traditional headmaster's academic gown. I took it down and placed it over my shoulders, straightening it in the mirror. If I may be permitted to say so, dear reader, I certainly looked the part.

There was a knock on the door and I shouted, 'Come.' The door opened and Andrea and Simone stepped in resplendent in their maroon uniforms, white socks and sensible shoes, followed by the policewoman. 'And what brings you ladies here,' I asked.

Simone spoke first, 'Errmmm, sir, I am afraid we were both caught shoplifting earlier, sir.'

I glared at her and looked her straight in the eye, 'Is that correct? Perhaps the officer would be kind enough to tell me what you took?'

Lucy stepped forward, 'Apparently, sir,' she responded, treating me with the respect that she would a senior officer, 'they both took both sweets and cigarettes, while the shop assistant's back was turned.

I found these back at their home, sir.' She produced 60 cigarettes and two Mars Bars from her pocket. 'This is the evidence,' she stated.

I looked back at Andrea, 'Do you deny any of this?' I asked.

'No, s…sir,' she stammered, 'I am very sorry, sir, but what she's saying is true.'

I looked coldly at the pair of them and said, 'At least you have the decency to own up, young lady, but you know full well that I cannot tolerate having the school's name brought into disrepute.'

'No, sir,' they mumbled in unison, now getting well into their roles.

'Sergeant,' I turned to Lucy, 'you may leave, safe in the knowledge that these girls are in for a very painful experience.'

'Thank you, sir,' replied Lucy, 'the shopkeeper and I knew we could trust you.' And with that she turned and left the room.

There were two school desks at the back of the room and I instructed the two girls to sit down, they only just managed to squeeze in behind them.

I laid a sheet of paper and a pen on each desk. 'You will,' I ordered, 'write out 50 times each in your best handwriting, "Young ladies who bring the school into disrepute deserve the consequences and pain they suffer as a result".'

I left them to it and sat behind the desk, picking up and starting to read a 1968 copy of *The Times* on my desk, that's how detailed the management there was.

Apart from the scratching of pen on paper, silence fell on the room. In a keyboard-driven age this was really a new experience for the girls. I had become quite engrossed in the paper when there was a loud knock on the door, 'Come!' I boomed again, really enjoying the moment. The door opened and it was Lucy again, but this time resplendent in her own school uniform, into which she had changed in the ante-room. She had a real rebellious teenage sulky look on her face, she was a good actress.

'Mrs Stephens sent me to see you, sir,' she almost sneered.

'And why would she need to do that, young lady?' I demanded.

'Because I punched that silly cow Anne in the face,' she responded, deliberately winding me up.

'You address me as sir, at all times,' I said. 'If what you say is true, young lady, then why isn't she here with you?'

'She's in the sick bay, sir. I think she may have to go to hospital.'

'In that case, young lady, you are in very serious trouble. Now stand up straight.'

I opened the Punishment book, flicked through it and then looked back at her, 'I see you were last here five weeks ago, Miss Archer. On that occasion you had been caught smoking, and I found it necessary to give you four strokes of the cane. I hope you have stopped?'

'Yes, sir,' she said sullenly.

'In that case,' I responded, 'you won't mind emptying your pockets onto the desk.'

She looked at me sheepishly as she took both cigarettes and matches out from her pocket and laid them on my desk.

'It's a double dose for you then, young lady, six strokes for having cigarettes in school for the second time this term, and then a further six strokes with my senior cane for fighting.' Andrea and Simone were gazing at us, transfixed by the scene unfolding before them and clearly more than a little nervous that they were inextricably part of it. Like rabbits caught in the headlights, wanting to run but unwilling and unable to do so.

'Miss Young and Miss Conway are in the same position as you, young lady, both about to face six strokes of the cane for shoplifting (I wanted to go easy on the younger less experienced girls, Lucy had told me exactly what she wanted), I may as well deal with the three of you together.'

'Yes, sir,' they chorused in unison.

'Miss Archer will go first, followed by Miss Conway and Miss Young, after which Miss Archer will take her second six for fighting. Miss Archer, please face the door and place your hands on your head until these girls have finished their lines. She turned and did exactly as she was told. I returned to my seat behind the desk and wrote out the sentences in the Punishment book, studying what had happened to the others who had passed this way before. I then asked the girls in turn to sign against their sentence in the book, using the blotting paper on the desk to dry the page before snapping the book shut.

I looked up some minutes later and noticed both girls had stopped writing. 'Have you finished girls?' I asked.

'Yes, sir,' they again spoke together, clearly not at all looking forward to what was coming next. I am sure they both felt excited and nervous as hell, just as they should.

Lucy by contrast was a much cooler cookie who had clearly been here before, even though she could have no idea about how my version of hard would compare to her regular Dom's, and she wanted to take what she was given with no safe word. I knew she wanted a real beating and that just watching it would scare the pants off the other two, who would then be expecting the same. The tensions were running very high.

I chose a junior cane from the rack and swished it through the air.

'Lucy Archer,' I announced, 'you know I don't tolerate cigarettes in the school yet here you are in my office with cigarettes for the second time this term.

'Bend over and touch your toes. Miss Conway, Miss Young, please both of you place your hands on your head and watch closely, it's your turn next.'

Lucy dutifully bent over, resplendent in her maroon skirt and white socks. She had solid muscular thighs as befits a very fit, not terribly thin, police officer.

I raised the cane and brought it down on top of her skirt with all the force I could muster. She let out a low squeal, the noise didn't worry me: the room was fully soundproofed from the outside world. Twenty seconds later I brought the cane down hard again, this time it was more of a grunt that she emitted. The two younger girls looked very scared.

Crack! The third stroke hit her squarely across the buttocks, she still hadn't flinched.

'Let's have your skirt up then, young lady.' I

pulled the hem of her skirt up expecting to reveal matching maroon knickers, but she was wearing nothing of the kind, a union jack flew defiantly at me, she had a sense of humour this girl.

I carefully took aim again and landed three further strokes in quick succession across the seat of her pants. She still didn't flinch, but as she stood up tears rolled gently down her cheeks. She sniffed loudly as she followed my instruction to place her hands back on her head.

'Simone Conway,' I announced, 'you are a thief, and thieves never prosper. You're not a girl I ever expected to see in this position and I imagine you allowed yourself to be lead astray by Miss Young. That doesn't mean that you don't have to face the consequences of your actions.' Her knees were shaking and I knew she wasn't going to make it touching her toes, so I decided to cut her some slack. 'Bend over the desk, young lady.' She did as she was told and on this occasion I raised her skirt immediately and tucked the hem into the waistband of her knickers.

She was wearing maroon knickers to match the rest of the uniform. Good girl.

A sharp flick of the wrist brought the first stroke arcing into her buttocks, just catching the sweet spot full on. She yelped loudly, she was trembling noticeably now.

I drew back and with an even sharper flick aimed the second stroke just two inches' higher. 'You should consider yourself lucky you are not getting additional strokes for the cigarettes,' I remarked as the third stroke sliced towards its soft target.

She was sobbing now, and continued to sob even

more loudly as the next two strokes hit their target. Should I be merciless, I thought, why not? She wanted the real experience, so a deft flick sent the last stroke flying into the soft flesh of her upper thighs.

She howled with pain, I stood and watched silently for a minute or so as the weal quickly turned from red to purple, before instructing her to stand up next to Lucy and put her hands on her head.

'Andrea Young ...' I announced. I looked closely at her. She was already beginning to go to pieces, having had to witness the two girls before her take what she was going to get, but she looked determined to go through with it, '... you are not only a thief but one who has been living on borrowed time, unlike Miss Conway I am surprised that you are here in this office for the first time today. It's not before time!

'I am sorry that you have to suffer the pain and indignity of this, but it will only be to your benefit in the long term. You need to learn the clear divide between right and wrong, and you should now be considering yourself very lucky that the shopkeeper did not insist on prosecution. I think you will agree that this is preferable to a criminal record,' I said gravely.

She looked at me almost speechless, before mumbling out the words, 'Yes, sir, you are right, I am very grateful, sir.'

'Then bend over the desk.' She quickly stepped forward and lent over the sturdy oak desk, 'Place the palms of your hand flat on the desk and keep them there until I tell you to move them. Is that understood?'

'Yes, sir,' her voiced quavered.

I immediately flipped up the hem of her skirt and tucked it in her waistband, she had her regulation maroon knickers too, which actually almost covered the tops of her thighs as well as her softly inviting buttocks. Not quite enough flesh on show, I decided. I needed to make adjustments and, having asked her to put her feet slightly further apart, I hoisted the knickers up into her crotch, baring a little more flesh and ensuring that the sweet spot was naked, the hem of her panties being just half an inch higher. It was a delightful sight and if all went to plan the panties would be down before I finished, but the option would be hers, as long as she could obey my instructions.

'Sir,' she blurted out, 'can I go to the toilet please? I'm about to wet myself.'

Of course I had to accede to this request and allowed her to stand up. She left the office and I was left looking at Simone and Lucy, both standing looking at me in something close to disbelief, with tear-stained faces and their hands still firmly on their heads. Andrea's procrastination was only making it worse for them, but it wasn't really her fault, although she was taking an awfully long time to return to the study. I was about to send one of the girls to fetch her when we heard the loo flush. The door opened and she returned sheepishly, her skirt hanging back around her knees.

'Right, Miss Young, let's have you back over the desk in *exactly* the same position as you were before,' I said. 'Let's get this over with, young lady, without further ado.' As I raised her skirt for the second time, I noticed that the panties were back in their original position too, it took me a further minute or so of fiddling to get her pants and bottom exactly back to where I wanted them, with her palms flat. Could she now hold this position? Only time would tell.

'Right, Miss Young,' I repeated, 'keep very still until I have completed my task, please understand that, should you move either your hands or feet, I shall have no option but to take your kickers down for the remaining strokes, and you wouldn't want that, would you?'

In fact, of course, I thought she probably would, I could tell that she was getting quite excited, the damp patch on her panties gave that away.

Anyway I was about to test her to the limit. I raised the cane and it swooped down hissing through the air and catching her buttocks perfectly, but it elicited only a little yelp. I quickly raised the cane again and delivered a second parallel stripe no more than an inch above the first, my accuracy was spot-on that evening. This time she winced more loudly, but she stayed perfectly in position, barely moving a muscle.

The third stoke was deliberately cruel, being aimed to land across the previous two strokes. It would have intersected with the lines of the two previous weals, predictably she yelled out loud this time and her right hand came up; she beat it three or four times against the table top. I imagined she hadn't really considered the consequences of that action, although, who knows, it may have been deliberate.

'I thought I told you to keep your hands flat, young lady. Miss Conway, can you help me out here? You may take your hands off your head and come here and hold Miss Young's wrists. Let's make sure she's not about to disobey me again, shall we?'

Simone moved around and took both of Andrea's hands in hers, they gripped each other tightly. Simone's hem line was still tucked in her knickers. They made a touching sight, two friends together in adversity.

I put my fingers inside the elasticised waist band of Andrea's pants and hauled them down to just above her knee, I could tell immediately from her moistness that she was, despite the pain, getting some pleasure from this. Behind my stern exterior, I was pleased, everything was working out well.

I admired her gorgeous young bottom for a few moments and then, stepping back to her side, I raised my cane for the fourth time; I wasn't going to kill her now. Firmly, but not excessively, the cane descended three more times, creating three parallel lines underneath the first two. I stood and watched as the weals turned redder and redder, but there was no purple this time. Only the third stroke had been hard enough for that, I knew. The weal it had left was angry and could well take a couple of weeks to fade, but I had needed an excuse to get her knickers down, hadn't I?

I told her to stand up and pull her pants back up.

While the girls were straightening their skirts, I turned my attention back to Lucy, who was still standing, hands on head, watching everything intently. I think she knew that for her the worst was yet to come.

I placed the Junior cane back on the rack and turned to face her.

'And now, Miss Archer,' I commenced, 'I have a

violent bully to deal with, and I think you know I always treat unruly violent girls as harshly as the school rules allow. It would be wrong to use the words young lady to describe you,' I said, pompously I must admit, but perhaps I was half starting to believe in my role and I was definitely enjoying myself – three beautiful aching young bottoms hung on my every word!

'Once I have finished with you I think you will be keeping your hands and fists to yourself in future.' I finished my speech, one I had, I confess to you, dear reader, rehearsed often enough in my fantasies. Lucy was great and just glared aback at me defiantly, she played the part so well. It suddenly struck me that it was a shame that all this wasn't being filmed.

The top cane on the rack was longer and thicker than anything I had ever used before. I had been told by the owner that it was a Governess cane: one step up from the Senior Cane and banned in all but approved schools and borstals even back in the fifties and sixties. A distinctly thuddy cane with little sting involved at all. He had cautioned me not to use it on anyone other than a very experienced pain slut; and then only with care if I didn't want to risk marking her for life.

When I first saw the rack of canes, and the Lochgelly tawse, I had had no thought of using this brute, but having seen Lucy in action I realised it was exactly what she wanted. I think I'm a pretty good judge of a woman's capacity to stand up to pain, indeed it's probably why, at the end of the day, I'm so popular, but sometimes a girl, when I see her in action, can surprise even me.

Lucy was that girl, she had told me she could take whatever came her way, of course I had taken it with a pinch of salt, but now I believed her. Also I felt that I had the level of expertise to use the Governess correctly, I picked it up and swished it, it was a good six inches, perhaps eight inches, longer than the standard senior cane.

Lucy gulped audibly and spoke to me, 'Are you serious, sir, are you really going to use that?'

'Yes. Yes … young lady, I am. Do you have a problem?' I spoke firmly but slowly, allowing her the time to put a stop to everything if she wished. I waited.

'No, sir,' she responded, quite firmly, 'I guess I deserve it!'

I stood up and faced her, 'Those are not regulation kickers, young lady, take them off immediately. They are confiscated, you can collect them from the secretary's office at the end of the week – hand them to me now.'

The Union Jack was quickly lowered to half mast and, finally, she took them off completely, handing them to me. I put them in my pocket, a trophy, a permanent memento of the evenings proceedings!

'Now unzip your skirt and take it off.' She obeyed instantly and hung it over the back of a nearby chair. She looked a real delight as she stood facing me: short brown hair, stockily built but very fit, her breasts straining against the confines of her white blouse and maroon sweater. I wondered if she had kept them from her schooldays, waiting for this moment, I realised that she was wearing her old school tie – how hadn't I noticed it before? She was particularly bushy down below, clearly she didn't believe in trimming, let alone a full Brazilian. I have to say her thatch looked quite absurd in contrast with her white school socks, although they did match the bikini shadow from her recent Caribbean holiday. Other than the white patch where her bikini knickers had been, she was very tanned. Indeed it gave me a perfect target.

I looked at Andrea and Simone, and said simply that I needed their assistance.

'Bend over the desk, Miss Archer,' I boomed, 'it's time for you to regret your stupidity.' Once she was over the desk I instructed the two younger girls to take an arm each and pin her firmly to the desk, she wasn't going to go anywhere.

I took my time to position myself this time, a little further back than previously, to take account of the longer cane, the tip still needed more than ever to touch the far buttock and not wrap around the hip: the Dom's worst crime.

Despite my not putting that much effort into the first stroke, the cane still hissed down towards its white fleshy target, connecting perfectly. Being a thicker cane, two narrow red tram lines appeared and the flesh between the lines turned very white, before reddening rapidly after about thirty seconds. The second stroke was a little harder and made Lucy gasp gently, but my aim was true and I was now ready and confident to go for it. Standing there in my academic gown, I finally knew exactly how our headmaster must have felt all those years previously, although he never had the joy of a naked adult female bottom to aim at, so I suppose this was still very different.

As I raised my cane for the third stroke, I really

prayed I was going to get this right. It was new territory for both of us, though I guessed she wasn't about to report me to the police if I got it wrong, too much explaining to do. Also she had assured me, over drinks, that she wanted a real harsh experience and I was to err on the side of severity with no comebacks from her side. Her husband was away with the Army for the next six months so she had time to recover!

Down the cane whistled and the two girls holding her had to grab her extra tightly as she simply emitted the word 'fffuuucccckkk' long and loud, she clearly had been taken to new and unexpected levels.

I waited almost a minute for the effects of the stroke to be fully seen, I wanted to see what damage I had caused before I proceeded any further. I had my limits too – as to what I considered sane and sensible – and this was getting very close. It's an amazing sight watching a cane mark first turn white as the blood rushes away from the skin's surface only to turn red a few moments later as the blood returns, and if you have really laid it on it will then turn purple-black very quickly. And, I saw, that stroke had indeed left a black mark within a minute.

'Are you all right, young lady?' I ventured, offering her the chance to quit even if we had agreed no safe words, but she responded pretty firmly that she was fine. What a brave girl, what a pain slut!

The fourth stroke landed with equal force just above the previous two, and she dissolved instantly into tears.

I really wanted to stop, I will confess to you, dear reader; I had finally met my match, but I knew she didn't want me to.

'Only two more, young lady,' I offered, 'and at least you won't end up at the hospital like your victim.' You may think that, at this stage, this was a bit unnecessary but in fact sustaining the fantasy at this point was vital.

How hard does one cane an already wailing woman? The answer was just as hard as the previous two strokes, no more, no less, but I made doubly sure I found a new tract of virgin white flesh to lay it on. It raised another shrill scream, I thanked God the place was sound-proof.

I angled myself slightly differently for the final stroke, looking at the 5 parallel black weals already spread across her cheeks, I aimed the final stroke to intersect them all, the perfect 'five-bar gate': I believe it was the most painful cane stroke I have ever given.

As Lucy screamed in pain, I replaced the cane on the rack.

Andrea and Simone released her, but she stayed lying across the desk sobbing for a full five minutes before she stood up. The younger girls helped her back into her skirt, she had no knickers – they were still in my pocket. Andrea helped to put her coat on as Simone collected her bag from next door; they were still smarting too but nothing like Lucy. I took my gown off and hung it back on the peg on the door before taking Lucy's arm and helping her down the stairs to my waiting car. The four of us drove silently back to the girls' flat and they went in, as I had previously agreed with Lucy, leaving me to drive home alone.

As also arranged I didn't contact them again till next

morning. I rang Lucy on her mobile phone and asked her how she felt. It turned out she was still at the other girls' flat, unable to sit, but totally unbowed by the experience. 'I am really glad I did that,' she told me, 'but I certainly wouldn't want to do it again, I have learned my lesson. It was good meeting you, though.' We had decided in advance that this would be a one-off encounter – that was her wish, part of her fantasy, and I knew I would never see her again.

Andrea and Simone, on the other hand, were still friendly when I popped by their flat that evening, and proudly showed me their vividly marked bottoms. 'I guess I know how Mum felt now,' Simone said, 'and I certainly will behave myself in future. I wouldn't want to go through that again in a hurry, and certainly couldn't face what Lucy did, she was amazing.'

'I think I owe you girls a treat,' I suggested as I was leaving, 'why don't I take you to dinner at The Savoy Grill on Friday? I have a reservation.' It was one suggestion neither of them was going to say no to.

ABOUT THE AUTHOR

IT ALL STARTED WHEN I was ten or eleven and I first encountered the swish of the cane. It scared me half to death and I wasn't even on the receiving end. An incident in which two boys in my class had tried to take a girl's knickers down had led them straight to the Head's office, which was next door to my classroom.

Twelve times we heard the swish of the cane and a sharp thwack, with a gap after six, when, no doubt, one boy stood up while the other bent over the desk. As the boys came back into class, fighting back the tears, I vowed from that day not to misbehave, to avoid the cane at all costs.

Even in those days, corporal punishment was not common, either at primary school, where there was only the odd incident, or in secondary schools, where its use was being phased out, but our headmaster did get his cane out a couple of times a term for the boys, just to remind everyone who was boss. But not for the girls, though!

Over the course of the next few years I didn't even come close to being caned, though we heard all sorts of stories from other schools.

But it wasn't to last, having been caught smoking

I was sent to the headmaster, as it was a caning offence in principle. I was pretty sure he wouldn't go that far, but my stomach lurched as I listened to him lecture me. He was disappointed, he said, I deserved to be caned, but he felt I was too old for it. If, however, my behaviour was brought to his attention again that term the outcome would be 'short, sharp and extremely painful, I am sure you understand me, Jones'. It struck me then how a single sentence could scare someone to the point where his knees knocked and the butterflies trembled, and, that day, they certainly did.

Two weeks later, I was minding my own business when one of the masters collared me in the corridor and announced he was going to take me to see the headmaster. Apparently someone had smashed a door off its hinges. I genuinely knew nothing about it, it was a case of mistaken identity, but there was no convincing him of it.

The Head, a large man in his fifties, told me to stand outside his door, hands on head, while the master went in to explain what had happened. I'm sure I turned white, my knees certainly were trembling, my stomach doing back-flips.

'Come, Jones,' a voice boomed from within. I knocked on the door, entered, and stood before his desk. He rose from his chair, and looked me in the eye.

'You know I don't tolerate vandalism, and you have been here already once this term. I warned you, didn't I?'

'Yes, sir,' I mumbled, desperately trying to decide whether or not to protest my innocence, knowing it could make things worse if I did.

'And what did I warn you with, Jones?'

'The cane, sir,' I mumbled, a bit louder this time, having decided it would be best to take what was coming and be over with it, surely it wouldn't be that painful. I was a big boy; I could take it. Maybe, just maybe, I had a subliminal urge to find out.

The head went to a cupboard and took out the cane; I hadn't even seen one before and it struck instant fear into me, it was much bigger than I had expected, almost three feet in length and quite thick, with a crook handle, still flexible enough for him to bend almost double.

'You've not been caned before, have you, Jones?'

'No, sir,' I responded.

'I am going to ask you to take off your jacket, and hang it over the back of that chair.'

I did, feeling almost naked, which was silly really.

'Bend over the desk, Jones.'

I took a deep breath and reached forward across the desk, the grey flannel trousers and the regulation y-fronts I was wearing suddenly feeling very thin.

I braced myself when I heard the cane start its trajectory, a split second later it hit my buttocks, at first nothing, but then a few seconds later the pain started and burned and burned; I had never felt such pain in all my life. I grimaced and kept as still as I could, 'thwack!' down came the second stroke, what seemed like an eternity later.

A second line of fire parallel to the first spread across my buttocks. By the time he reached six I had tears pouring down my cheeks, especially as the last

171

stroke had been aimed to bisect the first five and take me right out of my skin. The Gaffer certainly knew what he was doing.

I rose and was summarily dismissed, I put my blazer back on and tried to walk back to class in a dignified manner, knowing all eyes were on me. The girls looked sorry for me, but a few of the boys smirked.

I got no sympathy from my mother either when I got home; she merely expressed surprise that I had never been caned before. I lay on my stomach on my bed with my cheeks still burning mildly until I finally fell asleep. The next day it wasn't comfortable to sit. I had been caned, and I probably deserved it, if only for past misdeeds I had got away with! In those days, the late 60s, you simply accepted it.

Eventually I got to the upper sixth and was made a prefect, an authority I rather enjoyed, although of course dishing out the cane wasn't within my remit, lines and the odd detention were as far as I could go. I did start to idly wonder what it might be like to have the authority to use the cane, especially on girls' bottoms. I was seventeen and my hormones were at work, it struck me as an odd fantasy, though, one I should keep to myself. I did, but it never went away.

Then it happened: one of the girls in the fifth form, Jennifer Brooks, probably around sixteen years of age, got into a big fight. She was a well-known bully and it took two teachers to pull her off the girl she had attacked, who was left with a broken nose and blood everywhere. Any boy in that position would have had only one thing coming to him, six of the very best, but this was a girl and a very attractive sixteen-year-old whom we all had the hots for. What would they do? I lay in bed that night dreaming that they would give me the task of caning her, an unlikely fantasy. As it turned out, she had been expelled that afternoon.

By lunch time the school was abuzz with talk of how unfair it all was, boys like me who had been caned felt she had got away lightly, while most of the girls felt she should at least have been given the option of the cane rather than being expelled four weeks before her GCEs.

Her mother clearly felt the same; word went round that a meeting had been arranged with the headmaster the following morning. Eventually it was decided that Jennifer could resume her studies if she came back to school for a caning, to be administered by the deputy headmistress.

The following morning she slipped into assembly last, well behind everyone else. She was looking very nervous and all eyes were on her. At the end of assembly the Head read out the detention list as usual and then announced that Jennifer Brooks was to report to Mrs Armitage immediately after assembly. We all knew what that meant. I was on duty clearing books from the hall and tidying up after assembly so I watched through the glass door as she was ushered into the Head's office with her mother. I managed to get myself to a point at the back of the hall where I heard every stroke. Despite the closed doors, my imagination was running overtime and I had an erection like never before. In my mind, dear reader, I was Mrs Armitage.

*   *   *

The die was cast. I wanted to spank someone. I wanted that authority, but how could I get it? It seemed an impossible idea, no one would do it just for fun. It would, it seemed, be an unfulfilled dream, but one I masturbated over for years to come.

I passed my A Levels and, after a summer working in a holiday camp, I found myself at college in South London. Now I was part of the big metropolis, the world was my oyster, but where was the pearl hidden?

I encountered dozens of girls with pert bottoms that I would have loved to spank but unfortunately I didn't have the least idea how to approach them. I did have one discussion about spanking with my girlfriend of the time. When I raised the subject, she told me about a boy at her school who had been caned for an incident in which she had broken her arm; she believed it had actually been an accident and felt that the caning was barbaric. Not the best place to start!

I did, soon after, discover the magazine *Janus* on the top shelf of my local newsagent's, there hadn't been anything like it in my quiet country town. I was transfixed by the magazine's tales and letters about caned schoolgirls, girls being spanked for shop-lifting and stable girls getting whipped for turning up late to muck out the horses. There was nothing very consensual about these stories, but I did finally start to understand that, thankfully, there are people out there who do enjoy being spanked!

But where could I find them? I was a boy of twenty-one or twenty-two and it appeared that these girls, if they existed, as it seemed they did, were

174

looking for older experience spankers, not for me.

I did on a couple of occasions play-fight with girlfriends, getting them over my knee for a couple of slaps, but none of them seemed to particularly enjoy it.

I managed to have one long and intense conversation about it with a girl. I was sharing a flat with her at the time, but unfortunately she was a friend's girlfriend. She wanted to know all about the cane and corporal punishment and what it was like because, as a trainee teacher, she had that day sent a girl to the deputy headmistress and the girl had been caned. She had been mortified at first, but then thought that perhaps it wasn't so awful, perhaps she deserved it, she didn't know.

Have you been caned and how bad is it, was her simple question. I tried to explain as best I could, yes, it was excruciatingly painful, but, in my view, you soon got over it. Something to be avoided if at all possible, but still preferable to the more serious forms of punishment, expulsion from school or even approved school. I had heard tales of approved school beatings that even I considered barbaric. But there was a line between what was acceptable and what was not, and I'm sure the vast majority of schoolteachers never crossed it.

I was of course dying to suggest that she brought a cane home and that I try it out on her, then she could judge for herself. But I didn't have the courage, and, with hindsight, I doubt if I would have done a proper job of it anyway. As I was later to learn, (and so will you, dear reader!) there is a lot more to corporal punishment than just swinging a cane at a young lady's buttocks.

*   *   *

I soon met a girl who later became my wife, and still is. We did talk about it a little, one slightly drunken night, and I gave her a few sharp taps with my belt bent over the bed, having taken her knickers down first. She didn't enjoy it, not because of the pain, which must have been only slight, but because she simply got nothing from it.

A lot of women don't; however the good news, for me, is that surveys show that between 20% and 30% of women do, that's perhaps half a dozen girls in the average aerobics class. But how the hell does one find out which ones?

I continued to dream but knew it was never going to be more than that, a nice fantasy.

But the world moves on and, many years later, with a successful career in the legal profession under my belt, I finally decided I needed to treat myself to one of those new-fangled personal computers that everyone was suddenly getting. I had no idea how they worked or what they could do, but the man who sold me one gave me a swift lesson.

I knew about email anyway, as I had been using it in a limited way at work, but how did this surfing thing work? Simple, he said, just type in www.google.com and then type in a word or a sentence that you want to know about.

As soon as I got the computer to myself, when the family weren't around, I couldn't resist it, I typed in the word SPANKING, and my world was never going to be the same again.

176

More great books from $\boxed{\text{X}}$cite...

Each book contains twenty bottom-tingling stories to make your buttocks blush!

Miranda Forbes has chosen only the finest and sauciest tales in compiling these sumptuous books of naughty treats! Spanking has never been so popular.
Find out why ...

Naughty Spanking One - 9781906125837 – Price £7.99

Naughty Spanking Two - 9781906125899 – Price £7.99

An exciting collection of erotic stories with mixed themes
that are certain to please and tease!

ISBN 9781906125844 price £7.99

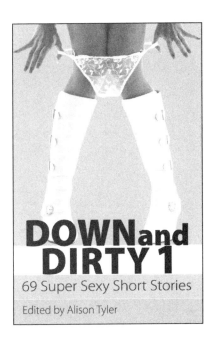

The short stories in this collection are written by some of
the best authors in the business – including M. Christian,
Thomas S. Roche, Sage Vivant, Maxim Jakubowski,
Rachel K. Bussel, N. T. Morley, Dante Davidson, and
many more. Some stories are sensational sexual snippets,
while others are fully detailed dramatic depictions. All of
the 69 pieces have one thing in common: they're dirtier
than dirty. And we know that's just the way you like them!

ISBN 9781906125851 price £7.99

For more information about
and to sign up for our
exciting newsletter
please visit

www.xcitebooks.com

Thank you!